Lady Rosamond's Secret

Rebecca Agatha Armour

Contents

LADY ROSAMOND'S SECRET

BY

Rebecca Agatha Armour

INTRODUCTION.

The object of the following story has been to weave simple facts into form dependent upon the usages of society during the administration of Sir Howard Douglas, 1824-30. The style is simple and claims no pretensions for complication of plot. Every means has been employed to obtain the most reliable authority upon the facts thus embodied. The writer is deeply indebted to several gentlemen of high social position who kindly furnished many important facts and showed a lively interest in the work, and takes the present opportunity of returning thanks for such support. In producing this little work the public are aware that too much cannot be expected from an amateur. Hoping that this may meet the approval of many, the writer also thanks those who have so generously responded to the subscription list.

Fredericton. August, 1878.
LADY ROSAMOND'S SECRET
A ROMANCE OF FREDERICTON.

CHAPTER I.
OLD GOVERNMENT HOUSE.

Breathes there a man with soul so dead,
Who never to himself hath said,
This is my own, my native land!--*Scott.*

A September sunset in Fredericton, A. D. 1824. Much has been said and sung about the beauteous scenes of nature in every clime. Scott has lovingly depicted his native heaths, mountains, lochs and glens. Moore draws deep inspiration amid scenes of the Emerald Isle, and strikes his lyre to chords of awakening love, light and song. Cowper, Southey and Wordsworth raised their voices in tuneful and harmonious lays, echoing love of native home. Our beloved American poet has wreathed in song the love of nature's wooing in his immortal Hiawatha. Forests in their primeval grandeur, lovely landscapes, sunrise, noonday and sunset--each has attracted the keen poetic gaze. Though not the theme of poet or pen--who that looks upon our autumn sunset can deny its charms? The western horizon, a mass of living gold, flitting in incessant array and mingling with the different layers of purple, violet, pink, crimson, and tempting hues of indescribable beauty; at intervals forming regular and successive strata of deep blue and red, deepening into bright red. Suddenly as with magic wand a golden cloud shoots through and transforms the whole with dazzling splendour. The bewildering reflection upon the trees as they raise their heads in lofty appreciation, forms a pleasing background, while Heaven's ethereal blue lies calmly floating above. The gently sloping hills lend variety to the scene, stretching in undulations of soft and rich verdure; luxuriant meadow and cultivated fields lie in alternate range. The sons of toil are returning from labour; the birds have sought shelter in their nests;

the nimble squirrel hides beneath the leafy boughs, or finds refuge in the sheltering grass, until the next day's wants shall urge a repeated attack upon the goodly spoils of harvest. Soon the golden sheen is departing, casting backward glances upon the hill tops with studied coyness, as lingering to caress the deepening charms of nature's unlimited and priceless wardrobe.

Amid such glowing beauty could the mind hold revel on a glorious September sunset in Fredericton, 1824. To any one possessed with the least perception of the beautiful, is there not full scope in this direction? Is not one fully rewarded by a daily stroll in the suburban districts of Fredericton, more especially the one now faintly described? If any one asks why the present site was chosen for Government House in preference to the lower part of the city, there would be no presumption in the inference--selected no doubt with due appreciation of its view both from river and hills on western side. Truly its striking beauty might give rise to the well established title of "Celestial City." Though unadorned by lofty monuments of imposing stateliness, costly public buildings, or princely residences, Fredericton lays claim to a higher and more primitive order of architecture than that of Hellenic ages. The Universal Architect lingered lovingly in studying the effect of successive design. Trees of grace and beauty arose on every side in exquisite drapery, while softly curved outlines added harmony to the whole, teaching the wondrous and creative skill of the Divine. The picturesque river flows gently on, calm, placid, and unruffled save by an occasional splash of oars of the pleasure seekers, whose small white boats dotted the silvery surface and were reflected in the calm depths below.

On such an evening more than half a century ago when the present site of Government House was occupied by the plain wooden structure known as "Old Government House," a group of ladies was seated on the balcony apparently occupied in watching the lingering rays descending behind the hills. Suddenly the foremost one, a lovely and animated girl whose beauty baffled description, espied a gentleman busily engaged in admiring some choice specimens of flowers which were being carefully cultivated by a skilful gardener. Bounding away with the elasticity of a fawn, her graceful form was seen to advantage as she stood beside the high-bred and distinguished botanist. The simple acts of pleasantry that passed shewed their relationship as that of parent and child. Sir Howard Douglas was proud of his beautiful and favorite daughter. He saw in her the wondrous beauty of her mother blending with those graces and rare qualities of the heart which won for Lady Douglas the deep admiration of all classes. Beauty and amiability were not the entire gifts of Mary Douglas. She was endowed with attainments of no ordinary stamp. Though young, she displayed uncommon ability in many different branches of education; shewing some skill as a composer and musician, also a talent for composition and poetry. With simple earnestness she placed her hand lovingly upon her father's shoulder, exclaiming "Papa, dear, I have come to watch you arrange those lovely flowers." "Well, my dear, you are welcome to remain. I am certainly complimented by such preference. You must allow me to acknowledge it by this," saying which, the fond parent plucked a white rosebud and fastened it in the snowy lace upon the bosom of his child. "Papa, dearest, one act of love certainly deserves another," exclaimed Mary, as she fondly pressed the lips of Sir Howard, adding "remember that you are my chevalier for the remainder of the evening. When you have finished, we will rejoin the company." Mary Douglas seated herself in a rustic chair and chatted in gay and animated tones while her father listened with a deep interest. The well tried soldier, the gallant commander at Badajos, at Corunna, the hero of many fierce conflicts, and the firm friend and favourite of the Duke of Wellington, listened to the conversation of his daughter with as much keenness as a question involving the strongest points of diplomacy.

"Papa, this garden will fully repay you for your labour. I do wish that I could understand and enter into the study of plants and flowers as you do." "Ah, my Mary," exclaimed Sir Howard in a deep reverential tone, as his thoughts went back to the days of his boyhood, "I had a kind benefactress, and I may say *mother* in my aunt Helena. She created in me an early love for flowers, and I have always cherished it. Often during my campaign in the Peninsula, the sight of a lovely flower would call up emotions that would for the time unman me for the raging conflicts of battle. I always look upon flowers as the trophies of God's grace. Mary, I trust you yet will be able to attend to the cultivation of Heaven's choicest offerings, and remember, that by so doing, you only contribute a small share in the beautifying of nature." Having enjoyed this strain of converse for some length of time, Mary Douglas rose, exclaiming, "Now, Papa, you are at my service." Sir Howard bowed, and offered his arm to his fair daughter. Together they went out, being greeted by the merry party still lingering on the verandah. "Explain, Mary," said the foremost of the party, "this breach of confidence and utter contempt of the necessities of your friends. We have been vainly waiting your appearance to join us in a walk, and now it is nearly time to dress for dinner." "Very prettily said, Lady Rosamond," replied Sir Howard, "but as I wear my lady's favour, you will grant me a hearing on her behalf." Pointing to the spray of mignonnette and forget-me-not which Mary Douglas had placed on his coat, he continued, "I hope that your company has employed the moments as profitably. We commenced with vows of love and constancy, then followed topics of general conversation, and ended on the study of flowers. With this explanation perhaps some of this goodly company might favor us with a like result." "I venture to say, your Excellency, that in the present instance, we might too clearly prove the old saying as regards comparisons," returned Lieut. Trevelyan, "and would therefore enjoin silence." "Ah, no, Mr. Trevelyan," said Miss Douglas, "we will not allow our claim to be set aside in this manner. We must muster courage in our own self-defence as an offset to your acquiescence, or else papa will wear his laurels very lightly."

"In the first instance," said she, "we were admiring the beautiful sunset, the soft outline of the hills, and the beauty of the landscape. Is that not worthy of describing, papa?" The eldest daughter of this distinguished family made this appeal with a face beaming with the enthusiasm of her deep appreciative nature. Anne Douglas possessed not the great beauty of her sister Mary, yet was a lovely and loveable woman, capable of inspiring deep regard. Sir Howard acknowledged by saying, that if she continued, the comparison would turn the weight on the other side. "Not yet, papa dear," said Miss Douglas, "you must hear further. We were speaking freely of our warm reception from the citizens, of the social resources of Fredericton, its commercial interests; and before you joined us, were planning to ask your assistance, by giving your views and opinion of Fredericton in its general aspect, as presented on your arrival." "Mr. Trevelyan," ventured Sir Howard, "I am sorry to acknowledge that the ladies have sufficient cause to charge you with desertion of your colours; but the end may not justify the means." "Ah, papa, your inference is indirect--you will not surely justify Mr. Trevelyan." "In the present state of affairs," exclaimed Sir Howard, in playful military tone, "the enemy is preparing for action. The only chance of success is thus--retreat under cover of fire, or fall back on the strength of defence." "Your Excellency has a stronghold in the enemy's quarter," joined in

Lady Rosamond, who had been seated at the side of Captain Charles Douglas, their eldest son. "Before testing the strength of our forces let there be a short truce, on condition that His Excellency will give us the desired information this evening," said Mr. Trevelyan, playfully endeavouring to conciliate Miss Douglas. At this moment Lady Douglas formed an attractive feature to the group. Her graceful form, dignity of gesture and gentle expression was a subject of admiration. Her winning smile was greeted by recognitions of deep and respectful courtesy on the part of the gentlemen.

"My Lady, fortune has at last condescended to favour me by your appearance among us," said Mr. Trevelyan, rising and advancing towards Her Ladyship, while a blush suffused his handsome face, hastily making its way with deepening colour, showing the clear and open hearted spirit of the young Lieutenant. "We now have hopes of a speedy restoration." Mr. Trevelyan then related the foregoing sallies to the fair arbitress, who listened with keen relish and enjoyment. "As I have arrived at this unfavourable moment," said Her Ladyship, "I will try to end the matter satisfactorily to all parties. His Excellency being one of the chief actors, shall forfeit his liberty by devoting an hour in satisfying the present demands of the company. Mr. Trevelyan also, will only extricate himself from his present position by giving one of his many excellent renditions from Shakespeare or any of the favorite authors. Do you not all agree to this decision?" As Lady Douglas glanced towards her daughter Mary, she read in those beautiful eyes a mischievous flash directed towards Miss Douglas. "If I judge aright there is yet another to be brought to hasty retribution," said the former. "Pardon me, but I think your Ladyship is rather severe," said the youthful lieutenant with a boyish flush of youth upon his brow. "I beg that the penalty imposed upon Miss Douglas may be something which rests upon her direct choice." "Treason within the camp," exclaimed Captain Douglas, in his military tone. "Trevelyan, beware, you are being caught in a pitfall." Lady Douglas smiled as she turned to Miss Douglas, saying "Mr. Trevelyan's request shall be granted, you can choose your own task of imposition, music, reading, or any other pastime." "The matter is settled, thanks to her Ladyship," exclaimed Sir Howard, "and I beg leave to withdraw to mature my views for the coming lengthy topic of this evening." The hour being announced warned the ladies to prepare for dinner, the group separated leaving the verandah to the romps of two favorite hounds, a spaniel, and a pair of tame rabbits.

While preparations are thus going on in the different apartments of Government House, a carriage arrives with its occupant, Mr. Howe, private secretary to Sir Howard. The carriage, a handsome one, is driven by a span of full-blooded Arabian horses; magnificent specimens of their species; proudly sits their owner in his costly equipage. As a man of wealth, high family, Mr. Howe occupied a prominent position in the household of the Douglas family. His coming is awaited with eagerness. Captain Douglas, his friend and companion, is at his side in a moment addressing him with hearty familiarity, "Howe, you are late. Has business been pressing? Takes some time to get reconciled to the hum drum of life in New Brunswick! Well, old fellow, send around the horses and we will yet have time for a cigar before dinner. Strange, I enjoy one better before than after. You know I am an odd bird in every sense. Was odd last evening at mess when we got the rubber." "Douglas, one thing is confoundedly odd." "How did the natives of New Brunswick ever impose upon the British Government to send a governor and a private secretary," interrupted Charles Douglas. "Ha, ha, ha," laughed the latter, with repeated and renewed attacks. "Howe, you have been baulked in some design to-day; perhaps the fair one smiled on another, or odder still, some rival is ready to exchange a few kindly shots." "Oh, Douglas, for Heaven's sake stop and save your breath for more interesting topics," exclaimed the latter. The secretary lit a cigar and sat down to glance over the contents of a letter. Muttering some irreverent expressions upon the writer. "Howe, you 'see through a glass darkly,'" yelled Captain Douglas, "to-morrow you will see face to face Major McNair and the sports of H.M. 52nd. It will be mightily odd if you do not give them a brush. Count upon me, too, as I intend to show in earnest what stuff Prince is made of." "One thing you show," said Mr. Howe, with a strange grin--"a desire to turn parson or priest. I might make a few suppositions without interruption. Perhaps you have been initiating yourself in the good graces of a Rev. Clergyman, by a few such quotations. Perhaps the church might take better in New Brunswick than the army. Douglas, with all your perhapses, you are a cunning diplomatist." "You certainly do me credit, Howe," said his friend; "I possess enough cunning to perceive that you are not in your native element this September 22nd, 1824."

The private secretary of His Excellency, Sir Howard Douglas, was a man of no ordinary stamp. He had ability and coolness; the last named quality had gained him much favour from the veteran commander, and a desire to retain his service. Tall, slight and athletic, Mr. Howe was foremost in all feats of physical sports. Horse racing was his greatest mania. Few could manage a horse as he, and fewer still could own one faster than his favourite mare, Bess. Quickly he rose to his feet with "Jove, Douglas, I feel angry with myself and everybody." "Then keep your distance, I beseech you," returned Captain Douglas, in his usual jolly manner. "Listen for a moment and hear my scrape," said Howe. "Down in the mess this afternoon we got talking,"--"horse, of course," said the Captain--"yes, horse," said the former, "and got mixed up into one of the greatest skirmishes ever heard of. Captain Markham swore and raged like a wild beast Captain Hawley bit his lips with anger, and when I tried to conciliate matters, they turned on me like a set of vipers. In fact, with two or three exceptions, they hung together and irated me in good round English, forward and backward with little regard to Johnson or any of the time-honoured lexicographers. It was a hot encounter. In spite of anger, I cannot help laughing, to think how they abused each other, and, in turn, united themselves into a general force, directing the fire of their battery upon me. By St. George of England, it was too much. Of Course this is only the beginning of a series of such demonstrations." "All's well that ends well," returned Captain Douglas, "a night's sleep will restore all to a former footing. Major McNair would frown upon any breach thus made."

CHAPTER II.
AMID THE HOUSEHOLD

The spacious dining hall of Government House now assumed an aspect of studied splendour. The tables groaned under the weight of tempting and delicious dishes. The culinary intricacies of Sir Howard's table were often under comment. Viands of all kinds stood on every side, while the brilliant scintillations from chandeliers--massive silver and sparkling glasses--were of wondrous radiance. Sir Howard, preceded by Mr. Howe and Lady Douglas, led his beautiful daughter to a seat at his side. Captain Charles Douglas was the escort of Miss Cheenick, the family governess, and companion of Miss Douglas. The remaining part of the company took their places in like order, thus completing the usual dinner party. None but those who have passed much time in the company of Sir Howard Douglas, and enjoyed his many gay and social dinners and parties, can form any just conception of the true worth and genuine goodness of this fine specimen of an English gentleman. The flashes of wit and graceful repartees, mingled with sound judgment and truthful dignity, characterized the nature of the gallant Sir Howard. He was ever on the alert to minister to the wants of others. No one was neglected within his knowledge or recollection. From his daughter beside him to every guest around this festive board, none were allowed to go forth without coming directly under his recognition. The stern realities of military life through which he had passed, had in nowise interfered with those social qualities which so endeared our hero to the hearts of all. In Lady Douglas, Sir Howard found a faithful helpmate, a loving wife and deeply affectionate and pious mother. Lady Douglas never wearied in watching and caring for the welfare of her children. No mother could be more amply rewarded in seeing her family grow up loved and honoured; her sons true types of gentlemanly honour; her daughters having all those graces which are desirable to beautify the female characters, and make woman an ornament in her family and in society. "Mr. Howe," exclaimed Sir Howard, glancing towards that personage, "you escaped a severe ordeal by being tardy this afternoon. You have proved that every rule has an exception, but I must be careful not to introduce any comparisons;" thus saying, his Excellency directed his smile towards Mr. Trevelyan. Seated beside Miss Douglas, the young Lieutenant once more heightening the effect of his handsome dark eyes by the deepening colour of his cheeks. "Come, come, Mr. Trevelyan, reveal what is hidden behind His Excellency's smile." "Pardon me, Mr. Howe," said Lady Douglas, "I am pledged to relieve Mr. Trevelyan of any further parley. A truce was effected until the compromise is paid this evening in the drawing room." "I thank your Ladyship," said the Lieutenant, bowing. "Then, Your Excellency, that theory falls to the ground at present," said Mr. Howe, "I am not classified as an exception." The secretary smiled as he thought of the cause of his tardiness, and the sport his revelation would make for the gentlemen, when the ladies had withdrawn. "My Lady Rosamond is rather demure," said Sir Howard, smiling upon that young lady with his truthful smile. "Really Your Excellency cannot forget that I have been studiously trying to avoid any pitfalls." "Ah, you cunning rogue, you are amusing yourself with the shortcomings of the party," returned Sir Howard, "this is unjust. We will demand some concessions from those members who have been drawing largely upon the resources of others." Turning to Lady Douglas, he added, "Your Ladyship will please bear that fact in mind, or rather make a note of it. Lady Rosamond Seymour and Mr. James Douglas will make amende honourable for past delinquencies, not forgetting Mr. Howe. Will add that the last clause be conditional." A general flow of conversation follows as the dinner progressed. Harmony prevailed throughout while humour and wit were salient points in many topics. The most remarkable feature, perhaps, was the absence of anything that could not be received by the most fastidious. All practical jokes or questionable remarks were discountenanced by the family of Sir Howard Douglas.

One of the members laying claim to your attention is the Lady Rosamond Seymour, a distant cousin to Lady Douglas, descended from that distinguished family of Seymours so conspicuous in the Tudor Period. Lady Rosamond was a character of rare distinction. Her Father, Sir Thomas Seymour, an English Admiral, a man brave, honourable, respected and admired. He had married Lady Maria Bereford, the daughter of an English Baronet, who, dying at an early date, left two sons and one daughter--the Lady Rosamond. Placed under the care of a maiden aunt, the young lady had the benefit of learned instructions. Sir Thomas was determined that his child should receive all possible pains in her education. Though displaying no uncommon ability, Lady Rosamond was studious and persevering, compensating for genius by never failing application. She made considerable progress in classics, literature and poetry. In mathematics she was deficient. "I will do my best," she would often say to her tutor, "but you know I never was expected to be a mathematician." Lady Rosamond was indeed beautiful. The perfect features of her oval shaped face were lit by sparkling black eyes, full, large and dreamy, sometimes bewildering one with their variety of expression. While residing with her aunt, Lady Rosamond had formed an intimacy with Mary Douglas, which increased as they grew older. Together they spent many happy hours, and never wearied in their bright day dreams thus woven together. Nothing could exceed the grief of those companions when it was announced that the family of Sir Howard Douglas was soon to depart for New Brunswick. Lady Rosamond was inconsolable, and after urgent entreaties on the part of Lady Douglas, Sir Thomas Seymour consented to allow his daughter to remain with them for two years, after which she would for a time assume the duties and responsibilities of his household. Hence, Lady Rosamond Seymour came to New Brunswick with the family of Sir Howard Douglas, and thus we find her the friend of Mary Douglas in Fredericton.

In after chapters will be found the reason for thus introducing Lady Rosamond. To return to the preceding narrative. After the ladies withdrew the gentlemen remained to discuss over their cigars and wine. Mr. Howe began by repeating the affair among the messmates of the 52nd, and the result of his friendly interference. The warmth of his passion was aroused and he vehemently exclaimed, "Trevelyan, I both regard and respect you as a gentleman and friend, and feel regret that you were so unfortunate as to become attached to one of the most dissolute and dissipated of His Majesty's Regiments." The secretary was about to proceed when he was interrupted by Captain Douglas. "Strong terms, Howe. Your case would in some instances demand redress but I repeatedly avow not if considered in the light of reason." Mr. Howe saw in the strange light of Sir Howard's eye that His Excellency would now give, in a few words, his decision with unerring judgment. "Gentlemen," said he, rising from his seat and casting successive glances at all, "Mr. Howe seems to feel that the treatment received this afternoon should justify his seeking redress from those military gentlemen. Would any here think it necessary to create a breach between the Regiment and ourselves, from the fact of their having, while under the influence of liquor, shewed an incapacity to treat a guest with becoming respect, being utterly indifferent to every feeling save that engendered by abuse of appetite? Do I state it aright Mr. Howe?" "Your Excellency is right," said the Secretary, "sometimes I see the foolishness of being hot-tempered, but never more than on this occasion."

"We can afford to laugh at the matter now, Howe," said Captain Douglas, "to-morrow you will heap coals on their heads with a vengeance." The company enjoyed a hearty laugh, in which His Excellency joined. "You may have cause to bless your stars that you were absent, Trevelyan," said Mr. Douglas, "as you might have been pressed into service against Howe."

Guy Trevelyan was indeed a young man of marked ability and much promise. His father, Colonel Trevelyan, was a brother officer with Sir Howard during the Peninsula campaign. For signal service he was rewarded by knighthood and the rank of Lieutenant-Colonel. Having obtained for his son, Guy, a commission in H. M. 52nd Regiment, Lieutenant-Colonel Trevelyan hailed with delight the tidings of his friend's appointment to the Governorship of New Brunswick. The Regiment was then stationed in Fredericton and St. John--headquarters at the former--with Major McNair in command, while the companies stationed at St. John were in charge of Sir Thomas Tilden. In His Excellency, Guy Trevelyan had a warm-hearted friend. The son of Colonel Trevelyan was dear to him. Many times Sir Howard looked upon his handsome boyish face, pleased with tracing the strong resemblance between father and son. The open, generous and manly disposition of the young Lieutenant shone in every lineament of his countenance. Guy Trevelyan was loved by every member of the Douglas family. Lady Douglas showed him daily marks of favour, making him at ease in the bosom of her household. Nor did our young officer abuse these acts of true kindness and personal privilege. Unassuming, gentle and affable Guy Trevelyan was more eagerly sought than seeking. Sir Howard admired his favorite, his diffidence and bashful coyness. "He is one to make a mark," said he. "Give me the disposition of Guy in preference to those aping and patronizing airs assumed by the majority of young gentlemen on entering the army." Once, on addressing Lieutenant-Colonel Trevelyan, he wrote the following: "Have no fear for Guy; he is a true scion of the old stock. His nature is truthful, honourable and sincere, not being addicted to those vices which ruin our bravest soldiers. He has endeared himself to our family, in fact, Lady Douglas would lament his absence almost the same as one of her own sons."

Having made this digression, thus introducing the principal members of the company, we will now ask the reader to follow the ladies into the drawing room. Government House drawing room was indeed an apartment of costly elegance. Richly covered and gilded furniture was arranged in stately profusion. Quaintly and gorgeously embroidered silken draperies were festooned with graceful effect. Rare paintings adorned the frescoed walls. Priceless cabinets, vases and statuary were grouped with artistic hand. Turkey carpets of the most brilliant hues covered the floor, while the flashing and almost dazzling light radiating from the massive chandeliers, made the scene one of surpassing grandeur--something almost incredible outside the lustre and surroundings of a kingly residence. Such is a correct picture of old Government House over half a century ago. Then it shone with true chivalric glory. Now with its structure and surroundings a dream of the past.

In the midst of her group sat Lady Douglas occupied in some fancy netting, while each lady had some especial task. "Miss Cheenick," said Her Ladyship, "will you be so kind as to assist Miss Mary in the selection of suitable shades of silk for this piece of embroidery. You will accompany her to-morrow after luncheon, as she is anxious to commence." "It is to be hoped that we will meet with success as, judging from the appearance of the stores in this city, there is not much to select from," said Mary Douglas, "but, Miss Cheenick, only think, it will be our first attempt at shopping in Fredericton." "How much better and more convenient if there were exclusive dry goods stores as in England," said Lady Rosamond. "It is rather amusing to see all kinds of groceries and provisions on one side, and silks, satins and laces on the other. Pardon me, mamma, if I use the expression of Mr. Howe, 'everything from a needle to an anchor.'" "Well, my child, you will agree that both are useful," said Her Ladyship, "but I am doubtful whether the last named article is to be obtained here."

At the close of these remarks, the gentlemen were received. Sir Howard, true to his obligation, had found a seat beside his daughter Mary. "Papa," she exclaimed, "my knight is true,--'A good knight and true.'"

"At Lady Douglas' suggestion, I am duly bound to disclose some views upon New Brunswick and its capital. In the first place, I must plead ignorance, from want of sufficient time to note the general aspect, features and surroundings. This is a primitive soil, populated and toiled by a primitive people. Agriculture is yet in its infancy, and no prospect at hand for the furtherance of this important calling. Well wooded land, fertile valley and pleasing variety, show that this should be the great and only resource of this country. What facilities are afforded to the farmer for the importation of produce, were this noble river to be opened up with steam navigation. In a year hence, if my life be spared, I shall be able to afford you some information on life in the back settlements, and the means resorted to by the settlers. At present there are only five roads in the whole Province; three of which you have seen, as they lead from this city in different directions; the one to St. John; also, that passing our door to Quebec; and the third which I shewed you last week as leading to Miramichi. The fourth leads to St. Andrews, a small seaport in the south-west; while the fifth leads to Halifax." "Pardon me, Your Excellency, I could not help observing that the condition of these roads pay small tribute to McAdam, or Telford, being a rapid and sudden succession of up hill and down dale." "One would need a vigorous constitution," returned Sir Howard, "to make a practical test. People do not have much traffic upon these roads, from the fact that the settlements are more numerous along the river, which holds out more advantages."

"Papa," exclaimed Sir Howard's favourite daughter, "How much I should like to accompany you on an expedition through the forests of New Brunswick." "Perhaps you may, when the roads are more accessible, when there will be established comfortable inns where one can rest and be refreshed. None will press me to give any further report of the country, when I make a guarantee to do so at some time in the future, when there will be, I trust, good progress made."

"Many thanks, Your Excellency," said Mr. Howe, in response to Sir Howard, and, "in behalf of the company, may I express a hope that your wish be realized in the future of New Brunswick's history. May this province yet rise in commercial prosperity and national wealth, and may New Brunswick's sons yet assume their proud position as Governors of the province." "Mr. Howe is growing eloquent," remarked Lady Rosamond, to Mr. Trevelyan.--"A conspiracy on foot," exclaimed Miss Douglas, glancing towards Lady Rosamond. "Now Mr. Trevelyan will play his part," said Captain Douglas, with mock solemnity.

The young Lieutenant selected a passage from "Cymbeline," receiving the gratitude and applause of the ladies, to whose repeated entreaties he also read an extract from "King Lear," commencing with the line "No, I will be the pattern of all patience." Guy Trevelyan's voice was full, soft and musical, having the power of soothing the listener; but when required for dramatic readings, could command a versatility that was surprising. Miss Douglas archly proposed to Lady Douglas her wish to join in a game of whist. Thus engaged, the remainder of the evening passed quickly away. Mary Douglas still retaining her gallant partner, having secured the rubber against Mr. Howe and Miss Douglas, warmly congratulated Sir Howard on their success. "Never despair, Miss Douglas," said Mr. Howe, "we bide our time." The secretary's carriage being announced, with smiles and bows he took leave, followed by Mr. Trevelyan, who accepted the proffered invitation.

CHAPTER III.
AN EVENING IN OFFICERS' MESS-ROOM.

Many of our readers are familiar with the old building still standing, facing on Queen Street, known as the officers' barracks. At the time when this story opened, this was a scene of continual festivity--life in its gayest aspect. Here were quartered the noisy, the swaggering, the riotous, the vain, the gallant, the honourable, and all those different qualities which help to form the make-up of the many individuals comprising the officers of H. M. 52nd Regiment. At no period, before or since, has Fredericton ever risen to such notoriety. Several enterprising gentlemen of this body in connexion with a few of the leading citizens planned and laid the first regular and circular race course, near where the present now is situated, under the management of J. H. Reid, Esq., and the members of York County Agricultural Society.

On the old race course it was no unusual occurrence to witness as many as a dozen races during the space of two days. Sons of gentlemen, both in military and private life, were the owners of thorough-bred horses, each claiming the highest distinctions regarding full-blooded pedigree. These were Fredericton's glorious days--days of sport; days of chivalry; days of splendour and high life. On the evening in question, a festive board was spread with all the eclat attending a dinner party. Some hours previous a grand assemblage had gathered on the race course to witness a race between Captain Douglas' mare Bess, and a celebrated racer introduced on the course by Lieutenant-Colonel Tilden, ridden by his groom. Much betting had arisen on both sides. Excitement ran high. Bets were being doubled. The universal din and uproar was growing loud, noisy and clamorous. The band played spirited music, commencing with national airs, and, in compliment to an American officer, a guest of Sir Thomas Tilden, finished off with Hail Columbia. Bess won the race. His Excellency, Capt. Douglas, in the capacity of aide-de-camp, Mr. Howe and Mr. James Douglas, with their friend, Lieutenant Trevelyan, stood on an eminence bordered by woods. Here Sir Howard watched the afternoon's sport with keen interest. He saw in the assembly many features to be discountenanced. None admired a noble animal better than Sir Howard, and none were more humane in their treatment. Captain Douglas entered more into the sport of the proceedings. His whole mind for the present was centered on the expectation of his noble little animal. In gaining the race he was generous to the last degree. Honor was the password in all his actions, while he gave his opponents that feeling which led them to thank him for an honorable defeat.

The occasion of Lt. Col. Tilden's arrival was always hailed with a round of festivities. This evening was the commencement, servants in livery were at every footstep. An array of butlers and waiters was conspicuous arranging the different tables. The grateful odors emitted from several passages presaged the elaborate dishes to be served. The rattle of dishes, clinking of glasses, and drawing of corks, hinted of the viands in unlimited store. While the above were conducted in the mess-room, many of the guests were as busy in their own private apartments making the necessary toilet for the reception. In the foremost tier of rooms to the left, facing the river, on the ground floor, is the one occupied by Lieut. Guy Trevelyan. He is brushing out the waves of chestnut brown hair which, though short, shows a tendency to assert its nature despite the stern orders of military rule. A shade passes over the brow of the youthful-looking soldier as he dons his scarlet uniform. His thoughts are not at ease. Guy Trevelyan feels a vague and unaccountable yearning--an undefined feeling which is impossible to shake off. "Well, Trevelyan," soliloquized he; "you are a strange old fellow; such a state as this must not be indulged amidst the stir and hurly-burly of to-night. I believe bedlam has broken loose." No wonder that Trevelyan thought so; for, at that moment, several noisy songs broke upon him--the barking of at least a score of dogs, the clatter of steps upon the pavement, and the practising of fifes and drums. Such a babel--a distraction of noises and shouts of hilarious impatience were amusing in the extreme. At the appointed hour, the usual ceremonies of introduction being passed, the company were at last seated. And such a table! Such an array that one would only get into difficulty by attempting to describe it. Captain Douglas occupied a seat to the right of Lt. Col. Tilden and received that attention which characterizes Sir Thomas. Mr. Howe, once more on friendly footing, was assigned a seat beside the incorrigible Captain Hawley, whose choice epithets produced such sensitive effects upon the ears of the secretary sometime previous. Major McNair, a brusque, genial, stout-hearted soldier, always ready to do the honors of the Regiment under his charge, had on his right Captain Hawkins, an American officer; on his left an American youth and nephew of the officer. The convivial resources of these dinners were of a nature sometimes loud, boisterous, and exhilarating. Though indulging in countless practical jokes, various scenes of carousal, revels, mingling with toast upon toast, cards and amusements, there was a general good feeling throughout the whole proceedings. Misunderstandings sometimes led to sharp words, but the intervention of a superior had a healing effect. In nowise did Lieutenant Trevelyan receive so many taunts from his fellow officers as for habits of moderation. They often dubbed him "Saint Guy, the cold water man," which only served to amuse the young Lieutenant. The attention of the American was often directed to Mr. Trevelyan, listening with deep interest to the history of the young man and his distinguished father. "Lieutenant Trevelyan is a gentleman in every sense of the term," said the Major. "There is no need of that explanation, sir," said the American; "it is written in bold outline upon his handsome boyish face. His father will yet be proud of such a son." "The words of His Excellency," returned the Major. In the flow of general conversation that ensued many pretty speeches were made by the military and responded by several citizens, gentlemen who were frequent guests at dinner. Sir Thomas Tilden arose, complimenting Captain Douglas on his success, hoping that they may meet soon on the same business. This called from the gallant and handsome Captain one of his most witty and humorous speeches, after which Captain Hawley sang Rule Britannia with the entire company in a deafening chorus. After a short pause, cries of "Howe! Howe!" Nothing short of an oration would satisfy. The secretary rose and delivered something which would take some investigation to classify either as an epic, oration, or burlesque. They wanted variety and such it was. A puzzled expression rested on Lieutenant Trevelyan's face as he tried to follow Mr. Howe in the lengthy harangue.

The band afterwards played "Hail Columbia," which was the signal for Captain Hawkins to respond. The American thanked the Commander and Officers of H.

M. 52nd Regt. for the marked hospitality and courtesy extended to him during his stay. Alluding to the feeling of dissatisfaction existing between the sister nations, he hoped to see a firmer footing established between them; and all former animosities wiped out forever. These and other like sentiments called forth loud applause, the band playing "The Star Spangled Banner." Speech followed toast and song until the hours wore on unheeded. Lest it might be considered an absurdity, we will not say how many toasts were actually made--not in water, either, on this occasion. The strongest proof of this fact was found in the dozens of empty bottles lying scattered in profusion upon sideboards, tables and floors, the following morning, as servants looked on in dismay. The task of removal is no slight task. Before the company breaks up let us take another glance at Lieutenant Trevelyan. In respect to his superiors the young gentleman still remained as one of the company. Though twenty-one years had lightly passed over our young friend and favourite, one would not judge that he was more than eighteen. His smooth and beardless face had the delicate bloom of a young and pretty girl. Dimples nestled in his cheeks playing hide and seek to the various emotions of the owner. Guy Trevelyan had not mastered his feelings during the "hurly burly," as firmly as was his wont. Relapsing into an existence half reality, half dreamlike, he was striving to divine the true state of his thoughts when called upon by Sir Thomas Tilden. "Here is Lieutenant Trevelyan, the Adonis of our Regiment, whom we cannot accuse of a breach of impropriety to-night, except it be that of reserve." "Come now, Trevelyan, you are in for a song," exclaimed a dozen voices, pressing around the young Lieutenant, in noisy appeals. Contrary to their expectations, Trevelyan did favor the company with a patriotic song, which drew forth stirring applause and made him the hero of the evening. "Well done, my hearty," exclaimed Captain Hawley, slapping him on the shoulders, shouting lustily, "Hurrah for Trevelyan, hip, hip, hurrah for Trevelyan." "Eh, old chum," muttered Lieutenant Landon, in incoherent and rambling speech, about "faint heart and fair lady." "As congratulations are at present the rule, I cannot make an exception," said Mr. Howe. "Thanks my boy for this, and may you soon have occasion for another." "And another," roared the crowd, taking up the last words of the secretary. "My warmest thanks, Mr. Trevelyan," said the Lieutenant Colonel, warmly pressing his young friend's hand. This last act of courtesy was more gratefully received by Mr. Trevelyan than the noisy demonstrations of his brother officers. Soon afterwards, guest after guest departed in various moods and in various ways; some making zig-zag and circuitous routes, while others were more steady in the bent of their direction. More definite description might be given of these parties than that pictured here. More details might be given of scenes of dissipation, when each member must "drink himself under the table," to achieve the respect of his fellows; but the writer forbears not wishing to expose the darker shades of the picture, allowing the reader full control of his or her imagination, if willing to go further. Suffice it to say, no brawls had marred the "jolly time." All went away in good humour, while the American was so loud in praise, that he almost wished himself an officer in H. M. 52nd Regiment. Having made his adieu, Captain Douglas took leave for his bachelor's quarters, held in the house on the site at present occupied by George Minchin, Esq., on King Street, whither his friend Howe had preceded him. In this building, was kept the Governor's Office, as well. Here Captain Douglas found himself, as the darkest hour that precedes the dawn reminded of approaching day. "Howe," said he, "sit down and have a chat for a few moments. What did you think of the affair? Of cousin Jonathan and his nephew?" "One question at a time, Douglas," said Mr. Howe, pulling out a cigar case and passing one to his friend. "In answer to your first, I may say that under the circumstances there was some credit for being merry. It happened at a deuced bad time, but Sir Thomas took his defeat manfully, while those animated volcanoes, Hawley and Markham were wonderfully passive--a fact we must attribute to Major McNair. The general melee and pow-wow in which I was so unceremoniously toasted, taught a lesson. Jove, the Major is entitled to an order if he can, by any means, reclaim any of the 52nd. But the most amusing of the crowd is Trevelyan, who reminds me of an Englishman in Paris. He is clear, too. The oftener I see him the more I find to admire. He has a stock of drollery in reserve, too. Only think of the song and how received; Jove, he can sing like a thrush or nightingale."

"Sometimes he wears a puzzled look which I cannot define; but Trevelyan one day will make his mark if not led astray by some of his comrades. Still, in the same youth, there is considerable backbone, plenty of determination if necessary." "Hold on, Howe, when are you coming to the second question," exclaimed Douglas, in slightly impatient tones. "Bide your time, old fellow. Getting sleepy too, by Saint George," said the secretary, using his favourite Saint and Patron as necessary expletive. "Oh! about Jonathan, or Sam, or cousin Jonathan. Cousin Jonathan is certainly a jolly fellow. How they did stuff him with compliments. Cousin Jonathan is a bigger man than when he arrived, and Markham, would you not think he hailed from the 'ould country,' by the quantities of that commodity supposed to come direct from Killarney, which he used upon cousin Jonathan and Hail Columbia. Ha, ha, ha."

"Douglas, the younger Jonathan is a genuine specimen of Young America. By Jove, to see him at good advantage he should have been seated beside Guy Trevelyan--our Adonis. Is not the old chap mighty complimentary? Think it was rather hard on the vanity of Landon and Grey. We must be sure give the toast to Trevelyan, when they are present, to have another skirmish." "Judging from your state of mind at the first, one would not deem it advisable to enter the lists a second time," said Captain Douglas. "Bear in mind the Major has too much on his hands already." "Constant practice only serves to sharpen his wits," said Mr. Howe, with a vein of sarcasm in his tones. "It grows late, or, I should say, early," said Douglas, without taking notice of the last sentence. "Howe, good morning, I shall retire." "Au revoir Douglas."

"Oh, sleep! Oh, gentle sleep! Nature's soft nurse," murmured Captain Douglas, as he sought repose from the wearing and fatiguing rounds of the last evening and remaining part of the night. Soon the "gentle sleep" was upon him, and, steeped in quiet forgetfulness, slept peacefully, regardless of toast, speeches and cousin Jonathan.

His friend in the adjoining room still puffed away at a cigar, drank another toast to cousin Jonathan, soliloquizing: "By Jove, I shall watch him closely. He is a clever youth, but I shall make a study of him. If he would make me his confidante I should readily assist him. Douglas has not the penetration to perceive it, but I can. Can any young lady be mixed up in the affair? If so, I may be at a loss to discover." In the meantime, the secretary, now thinking it time to follow Douglas to gentle sleep, commenced to prepare for retiring, further soliloquizing: "That look puzzled me last night, I must make good my word." Here he stopped short and was soon enjoying sound sleep, in order to feel refreshed for the duties and social demands of another day. The coming day intended to be almost a repetition of the past. Morning, public parade; afternoon, on the race course; and evening in the mess-room.

Sir Thomas Tilden's arrival was always hailed with joy, being marked with grand festive honours, balls, parties and suppers. To these seasons the officers and many of the leading citizens looked forward with fond expectation. Beautiful ladies met in their ball-room the gallantry and chivalry of Fredericton. Nothing but gaiety on every hand. Such events marked the order of society in the capital of New Brunswick over half a century ago.

CHAPTER IV.
LADY ROSAMOND'S REVERIE.

In a small but exquisitely furnished apartment in Government House sat a young and beautiful lady. The room commanded a north-west view, showing a bright and silvery sheet of rippling water. This was the private apartment of Lady Rosamond. It is the hour when she is occupied in writing letters and attending to the many little matters demanding her attention. An open letter lies upon her lap. Lady Rosamond is listlessly leaning against a dressing-table, with one hand partially shading her beautiful face. Quickly turning round to look at some object beyond gives a full view, which reveals a tender sadness resting in the depths of those powerful dark eyes. Lady Rosamond is in a deep study--one which is not of an agreeable nature--one which she is not most likely to reveal. Alternate shades of displeasure, rebellion and defiance, flit across her brow, which remain, in quiet and apparently full possession, until reluctantly driven forth by the final ascendancy of reason, at the cost of many conflicting feelings of emotion and deep despondency.

Again Lady Rosamond reads the letter very slowly, as though to find, in each word and sentence, some other meaning which might allay her present distracting thoughts. Vainly did the reader search for relief. The diction was plain, clear and definite. No chance to escape. No fond smiles from Hope's cheering presence. Hope had fled, with agonizing gaze, as Lady Rosamond once more read that letter. Every word was stamped upon her heart in characters of bold and maddening outline. Heaving a deep sigh she folded the letter, placed it within her desk, and mechanically stood gazing upon the quiet river, peaceful and calm, save the little ripple on the surface. Lady Rosamond contrasted the scene with her troubled depths and superficial quiet exterior.

Quietly opening the window the cool sharp breeze of an October morning was grateful to the feverish flush partially visible upon the cheeks of Lady Rosamond. She was usually pale, save when an occasional blush asserted its right. Standing here in such a state of mind Lady Rosamond was indeed beautiful--a lovely picture with delicate expression and coloring. While she is thus engaged let us intrude upon the privacy of her feelings by taking forth the letter from its hiding place, and examining its contents. It seems a sacrilegious act, but it is in our great sympathy and interest on behalf of Lady Rosamond that we yield to the temptation.

The writing is in a bold, masculine hand, clear, legible, and uniform. If there be such a thing as judging the character of the writer by the chirography in the present instance, there was decision, firmness, bordering on self-will, and resistance to opposition. The letter ran thus:--

Chesley Manor, Surrey, Oct. 4th, 1824.

My Dear Child:

Having a few moments to spare this morning I devote them to your
benefit, with a fond hope that you are as happy as the day is long.
It does seem rather hard for me to be moping around this quiet
house and my little girl away in New Brunswick, but it is useless
to repine. In a few days I will take charge of a ship to go abroad
for some months. Our fleet now demands my attention, which, I am
happy to say, will drive away loneliness and repinings for the
little runaway. Was much pleased to meet an old friend of Sir
Howard Douglas--Colonel Fleetwood--who served in the same regiment
while in Spain, and is ever loud in praise of his friend. Though an
old soldier now, he has the true ring of military valor, which
would gain the esteem of Sir Howard.

Your aunt is enjoying a visit to Bereford Castle; writes in good
health and spirits. Your cousin, Gerald, is again on a political
campaign, being sanguine in the prospect of being re-seated in
Parliament the next session. I am watching the event as one which

concerns us deeply. Bereford is a young man of much promise. He will indeed fill well his position as owner of Bereford Castle, as well as peer of the realm. Lord Bereford is truly proud of his heir as the noblest of this ancient and loyal family. My dearest child, it is my fondest desire that in you may be doubly united the families of Seymour and Bereford. Gerald is the son-in-law of my choice, and it is my earnest desire that you may favor a fond parent's views in this matter. That your cousin regards you both fondly and tenderly I am truly convinced. He expressed his opinion very freely on making a visit last week, when I gave him my unbounded confidence and direct encouragement. On leaving he requested me to intimate this feeling towards you in a quiet manner, which I now do, with sufficient knowledge of your character to know that a parent's wishes will not be opposed. Gerald Bereford will be in a position to give you that ease and affluence your birth demands. As Lady Bereford, Lady Rosamond Seymour will neither compromise rank, wealth, nor dignity, and will be happy in the love of a fond, devoted husband, and the blessing of a doting father. It is my great love for you, my child, that urges this settlement. I am certain that you will have no hesitation in giving your answer. You are young, and have as yet formed no prior attachments, for which circumstance thank heaven, and allow me to congratulate you for being so fortunate as to secure the heart and hand of Gerald Bereford. Do not imagine that it is our wish to shorten your stay in New Brunswick. You are at liberty to enjoy the companionship of your friend Mary till the years have expired, after which I think that my daughter will be anxious to see her only parent, and to form high opinions of her cousin Gerald. My dear, I do not wish to hurry you, already knowing your answer. Wishing to be kindly remembered to Sir Howard and Lady Douglas, and the family, with my fondest love.

Remain, Your Father.

Such was the tenor of the epistle which had caused these feelings within the bosom of Lady Rosamond. Sir Thomas Seymour was a man not to be thwarted in his designs. He loved his child with deep tenderness, and, as he said in the letter, this was the reason of his solicitude. It had always been the secret pride of the Admiral's life that Gerald Bereford should wed Lady Rosamond, but he kept his favorite plans closely guarded until means were offered to aid him. Many times Sir Thomas fancied that Gerald Bereford admired his lovely cousin, and had a faint hope in the realization of his wishes. When the climax was reached, by those avowals on the part of the suitor, the great joy of the solicitous parent knew no bounds. He seemed to view the matter as one which would give entire happiness to all parties. Lady Rosamond was to be congratulated on the brilliant prospects of her future. The Bereford family were to be congratulated on their securing such an acquisition as Lady Rosamond, while Gerald Bereford was to be congratulated on having won the heart of such a pure and lovable being as his future bride. All those congratulations were in prospect before the mental vision of the Admiral as he lovingly dwelt upon the matter.

From the effect thus produced upon Lady Rosamond it was certain she viewed the matter in a different light. True, she had never, by thought or action, been betrayed to show the least possible regard or preference towards any of the many gallants from whom she oftentimes received many flattering attentions.

Towards her cousin Gerald she had always been considerate and friendly. When on several occasions he had taken particular pains to gratify her slightest wish, and pay more deferential regard than was necessary to the demands of their relationship, Lady Rosamond affected utter ignorance of the cause by treating him with a familiarity that gave him no opportunity to urge his suit.

When Sir Thomas gave consent to his daughter's reception in the family of Sir Howard Douglas, it was in the firm belief that on her return her mind would be matured to enter more fully upon plans relative to her settlement in life. At the death of Sir Thomas the lands and estate of Chesley Manor would be inherited by Frederick Seymour, the eldest son; a smaller estate, bordering upon that of Lord Bereford, affording a moderate income, went to the second son Geoffrey, while an annuity of four thousand pounds had been settled upon Lady Rosamond, with a marriage jointure of fifty thousand pounds, to be placed in the hands of the trustees.

By the marriage of Gerald Bereford and Lady Rosamond, the latter would secure an inheritance of which she was next direct heir, being the niece of the present lord incumbent.

Lady Rosamond weighed all these arguments and tried to find by some means a possibility of escape, but all lay in the dark and dim distance, exacting heavy payment from her ladyship.

This was a heavy blow to a person of Lady Rosamond's sensitive nature. The thought was revolting to her. For some time previous a dim foreboding haunted her--a presentiment of gloom and of deep sorrow. On receiving the letter its weight seemed to lie heavily upon her. Now the contents again caused her much pain. To whom could she go for comfort? To whom unburden her mind? Leaning her head upon the table Lady Rosamond sought refuge in tears. She sobbed bitterly. "It is at this trying moment I miss my dear mother," murmured the poor girl in faltering accents of outspoken grief. "Heaven pity those who have no mother. With her loving and tender heart my mother never would have allowed the sanctity of my feelings to be thus invaded and trampled upon. And my dear father, I love him, but can I fulfil his wishes? It is my duty! Oh, heaven direct me!"

Poor Lady Rosamond! Her sorrow was indeed deep. In the midst of such murmurs she arose, walked to the window, and once more fanned her cheeks with the cooling breath of heaven, which afforded momentary relief.

As the large plate mirror opposite reflected the tear stains upon her pale but lovely face, Lady Rosamond resolved to banish all traces of sorrow. Returning from the adjoining dressing-room not a shade clouded the features of the suffering girl. The silken ringlets of her raven black hair were rearranged with bewildering profusion, while the feverish blush added to her surpassing charms. A faint smile passed over Lady Rosamond's features as she tried to appear gay and assumed those girlish charms which made friends on every side, from Sir Howard to the youngest member in the household. "Oh, dear, what shall I do?" escaped the lips of the sufferer. "What will bring this matter to an end?" But pride would not allow Lady Rosamond to reveal her feelings. She would be a true Seymour. It were well that she possessed this spirit, being in this instance an offset to injured delicacy.

Having remained in privacy longer than it was customary, she reluctantly prepared to meet the family. Descending the upper stairway, she was met by one of the children who had come to summon her to join them in a walk.

Lady Rosamond was always a favorite with children and the family of Sir Howard formed no exception. They loved to accompany her on long walks in search of any thing the surrounding woods afforded. Scarce two months had passed since their arrival and they were familiar with all the cosy retreats, nooks and pretty spots to be found. Surrounded by her followers, Lady Rosamond appeared as a naiad holding revel with her sylvan subjects.

In her present mood the woods seemed to suggest calm. With her companion, Mary Douglas, and the romping children, Lady Rosamond was seemingly happy. A slight accident occurred which somewhat disturbed the enjoyment of all, more especially those whom it most concerned.

In crossing a narrow brook by means of a small plank which, being rotten, gave way, Lady Rosamond was thrown into the water with no regard to ceremony. A loud scream from Helen Douglas, who was standing near, brought the whole company, while terrified shrieks arose on all sides. In an instant Master Johnnie Douglas appeared in sight followed by Lieut. Trevelyan. The mischievous disposition of the former could not prevent an outburst of laughter despite all his high notions of gallantry. The young lieutenant came boldly forward, seized the hand of Lady Rosamond, and led her to a seat at a short distance. The dripping garments clinging to the form of the frightened girl moved the young soldier with pity and showed the tender nature of his manly heart. The heartless Johnnie was dispatched for dry wraps and more comfortable clothing. Lieutenant Trevelyan could not force a smile. The same puzzled expression which had baffled Mr. Howe forced itself upon him.

Mary Douglas had wrapped her companion's feet in the shawl taken off her own shoulders, and sat anxiously awaiting their courier. The children were more demonstrative in showing their grief. During the moments that passed the minds of the elder members of the group were busily engaged.

Lady Rosamond, regardless of her situation, was busied in projecting schemes the most fanciful. She was thinking of the contents of her father's letter. In spite of the strong efforts of will her thoughts would turn in another and far different direction, which, perhaps, on this occasion it would be more discreet to conceal. The painful and ill-disguised look was attributed to the accident. Well for Lady Rosamond if it were so. Yes, an accident, a painful accident--forgive the expression--an accident of the heart. Poor Lady Rosamond!

Ah, Mr. Trevelyan, we have an undue curiosity to follow the turn of *your* thoughts; but, as we once more note that puzzled look, think your generous heart and honest nature deserve more *generous* treatment. At least, this time, we grant you further respite.

Johnnie's arrival prevents further moralizing. No room for gravity when Johnnie Douglas is near. His mischievous spirit is infectious.

CHAPTER V.
CHRISTMAS FESTIVITIES, ETC.

The months pass quickly away. October, with its brilliant trophies of the wood, has departed, leaving behind many pleasing memories of its presence. November, in its raw and surly mood, is allowed to take farewell without any expression of regret. The last of this numerous family--December--is greeted with a hearty reception from every member of the Douglas family. The purity of the soft snow flakes, falling in myriads, are invested with indescribable charms. The clear, cold, and frosty atmosphere is exhilarating to the bright, fresh countenances of the youthful party sliding on the ponds and brooks. The river affords amusement for skaters. The jingle of the bells is music sweet and gratifying as the horses prance along with a keen sense of the pleasure they afford to the beautiful ladies encased in costly furs and wrapped in inviting buffalo robes.

A happy season is in prospective. Christmas is approaching with its time-honored customs and endearing associations. High and low, rich and poor, have the same fond anticipations. In the lowly cot, surrounded by miles of wilderness, little faces brighten as quickly at mention of Christmas as those who are reared in the lap of luxury and expectant of fond remembrance in showers of valuable presents in endless variety.

Preparations were being commenced at Government House on an extensive scale. Lady Douglas was remarkable for the labors of love in her family at this approaching season. Christmas was to her a time of unalloyed happiness. "Peace and good will" reigned supreme. Every minute was spent in promoting happiness by devotion, recreation or charity. The last was one of her most pleasing enjoyments, for which Lady Douglas received many blessings. From her childhood this noble lady had exercised her leisure moments in relieving the wants of the poor, often leaving to them food and clothing with her own hands.

At the suggestion of Miss Douglas, who was always ready for any important duty, a party was proposed to visit the woods to procure boughs for greening the grand hall and drawing-room. Foremost was Johnnie Douglas, master of ceremonies, whose presence on the occasion was indispensable; so said Johnnie, throwing a mischievous glance at Lady Rosamond as a reminder of his services on a former expedition. The rising color on his victim's face brought a reprimand from Mary Douglas.

"Don't be of such importance, Johnnie, there are plenty of gentlemen at our command."

"Ha, ha, ha," roared the young gentleman in undisguised and unsuppressed fits of laughter.

"Miss Mary, don't be of too much importance; there may not be so many gentlemen at your command as you reckon on," said Johnnie, bent on following up his argument; "Mr. Howe is engaged, Mr. Trevelyan goes on parade this morning, Charles is away; now where are the reserves? Answer--Fred, and your humble servant."

"Well, Johnnie, you are holding your ground manfully," exclaimed Sir Howard, smiling as he passed through the group in the lower hall, where they still sat discussing the grounds of Johnnie's superiority.

Decision turning in favor of the champion, the party set off--boys, ladies, and children--forming a pretty sight. Lady Douglas stood on the balcony waving approval and beaming with happy smiles.

The shouts of Master Johnnie, laughter of the ladies, and romping of the children, kept the woods busy in the constant repetition of echoes on every side.

"Oh, Lady Rosamond," cried the hero of the expedition, eager to maintain his position, "here is the brook, but where is the water to receive some one with another cooling reception, and where is Mr. Trevelyan with his gallant service and kind sympathy?--Not hinting of the hasty retreat of your valuable pioneer!"

Mary Douglas, detecting a shade passing over Lady Rosamond's brow, came to the rescue with another mild reprimand upon the incorrigible Johnnie. "I am afraid, sir, that you take the opportunity of reminding Lady Rosamond of your former importance without due regard to her feelings, which, you are aware, is not very gentlemanly."

"If your ladyship is offended," said the mischievous but generous and manly Johnnie, turning to Lady Rosamond, "I beg your pardon in the most humble manner, feeling deeply sorry."

"Lady Rosamond you really do not think I would consciously give you annoyance," said master Johnnie, throwing down the bough which he had lopped from a tree near, and drawing up his boyish form with true dignity and an amusing earnestness in his tone.

"Of course not, Johnnie," returned her ladyship, "you and I are on the best of terms. Nothing that you say or do gives me any annoyance; on the contrary, it always amuses me."

This last speech of Lady Rosamond had surprised Mary Douglas. Apparently engaged in selecting the most suitable branches of fir and spruce, she was more intently occupied in the study of her own thoughts. She was wondering why the mention of the brook adventure had caused that look which, notwithstanding protests to the contrary, recalled something disagreeable to Lady Rosamond.

Being interrupted in these thoughts by her brother Fred's arrival with a request to go home, Mary Douglas joined the merry party, each bearing some burden as part of the spoil, while Johnnie collected and piled a large heap to be conveyed thither when necessary.

On arriving in the courtyard, Johnnie set up three lusty cheers which brought out Lady Douglas, accompanied by Mr. Howe and Lieutenant Trevelyan.

"Thought you were on parade this morning, Mr. Trevelyan," exclaimed the pioneer Johnnie, "else you might have formed another of our party."

"The ladies might not have accepted your decision," returned Mr. Trevelyan, hastily; "however, I thank you kindly for your consideration."

After the ladies had returned from making the change of toilet necessary upon the tour of the woods, luncheon was served. Mr. Howe and Mr. Trevelyan remained. Johnnie was full of adventure, but made no allusion to the brook. Lady Rosamond was calm, possessed, and entertaining. Everybody seemed inspired with the occasion. Sir Howard was deeply immersed in the furtherance of those measures and means to be resorted to for the benefit and advancement of the Province. "I have promised," said he, "to be able to give clearer views upon the improvement of New Brunswick a year hence, and, in order to do so, must not neglect one moment. Another object which claims my notice very urgently is the establishment of laws regulating a better system of education. The grammar school is in a state of mediocrity, its support not being secured on a proper basis. We want a college--an institution where our young men can receive a thorough education and be fitted for entering upon any profession."

In every measure advocated by Sir Howard he had the full concurrence of Lady Douglas and her intelligent and highly educated sons and daughters. Perhaps to this cause may be attributed the amazing success which marked Sir Howard's career through life. He had the entire and heartfelt sympathy of his household. He was loved with the truest and fondest affection as a husband and father. He, in return, placed every confidence in his lovely and amiable wife and daughters, knowing that through them he received great happiness; and, unfettered with those domestic trials which attend some families, he was able to discharge the duties of state with full and determined energy.

The hours that elapsed between luncheon and dinner were spent in the various styles of decoration suggested by Lady Douglas. The important Johnnie was under the direct supervision of Miss Cheenick, cutting off and preparing little twigs for garlands, with occasional sallies of good natured badinage.

Miss Douglas was making illuminated mottoes and texts in a quiet corner of the apartment. Mary Douglas and her companion were busily weaving pretty and graceful festooning. To each member was allotted some especial part.

Every one participated in the preparation by noting each successive step towards completion. Thus the work progressed until it was time for the ladies to dress for dinner; after which the evening was spent in the same occupation, with the valuable assistance of Mr. Howe and Captain Douglas.

After several days had elapsed, the work was considered complete. The design was choice and beautiful. Nothing was necessary to produce a more graceful and pleasing effect. Holly there was none, but our woods supplied the loss with lovely evergreens of native growth.

It was the day preceding Christmas eve. Mirth and joy revelled around the glowing firesides. Happy faces beamed with radiating smiles. Each was trying to do some small act of kindness for the benefit of the household. A Christmas tree, in all its mysterious surroundings, was being laden with beautiful presents. Loving tokens of friendship were placed on its strong branches by lovely and delicate hands. Lady Douglas presided over these mysteries, in the secret chamber, with the vigilance of the dragon who guarded the golden apples in the classic shades of the Hesperides. All busy little feet were turned towards the door, but further entrance was barred by gentle admonition from her ladyship.

Lady Rosamond had been allowed the privacy of her own apartments without interruption. She was preparing some tokens of regard for different members of the family. Many chaste and valuable articles had been received from home for this purpose, but she wished to make some choice trinkets as her own work. Many times she had stolen a half-hour to devote to this labor of love. An elegant silk purse had been netted for Lady Douglas. For Mary Douglas she is engaged on a prettily-designed portfolio. None were forgotten, not even Sir Howard, who was the recipient of a neat dressing-case. As Lady Rosamond's deft fingers wrought upon each article her mind was busy upon a far different, and, to her, important matter. She longed for sympathy and advice. Her father gave himself little concern regarding her ambiguously-written message. He saw that his daughter was somewhat cold and indifferent to her cousin's preference, but he expected that, on her return, she would readily agree to anything which met his approval. Not wishing to repeat the sentiment of the letter thus described, Sir Thomas Seymour had considered moderation as the surest hope of success. Having thus expressed his opinion to Lady Bereford, the Admiral was assured and confident. On this Christmas season he had selected a costly locket, studded with diamonds, as a gift to Lady Rosamond, and dwelt, with loving pride, upon the many gentle qualities of the lovely girl; her happy prospects as Lady Bereford, adored by a fond husband, beloved by all.

Happy Lady Rosamond! in thy busy thoughts. Dared we venture for thee an encouraging word, it would be "Every cloud has a silver lining."

Christmas eve was a scene of stir and excitement. Though work was done in a systematic manner, the unusual tasks of labor and love were hurrying upon each other with increasing rapidity. The servant's hall was not to be passed over at this joyous time. Everyone, both family and servants, shared in the festivity. How the graceful form of Mary Douglas flew from room to room, arranging some pleasing surprise, planning some little act of courtesy or civility. The housekeeper's room, stealthily invaded by bribing another domestic, becomes the hiding place of a handsome lace cap. Each maid finds under her pillow a sovereign and some little trinket, as a ribbon, scarf or work box.

These were happy moments in the life of Mary Douglas. In the performance of such acts of goodness she was truly happy. This lovely girl was possessed of the united virtues of Sir Howard and Lady Douglas. Free from the remotest clouds of sorrow or care, Mary Douglas was indeed to be envied. Her father's smile was of more value to his gifted daughters than the most flattering attention from the many admirers who vainly tried to receive the slightest sign of encouragement.

That Lady Rosamond often longed for the happy and contented hours of her companion--for a like participation of uninterrupted and halcyon days, should form no ground for surprise. "How I should like to tell Mary my trouble and receive her sweet counsel," murmured the sad girl. "I should feel the burden lighter to bear, but it would seem almost a sacrilege to invade upon such quiet harmony, for, with her sweet sympathizing nature, I know that Mary would grieve over my sorrow. Dear girl, your Christmas shall not be clouded by me," soliloquized Lady Rosamond, "I love you too deeply to wish you care like mine. Ah, no, Mary darling, may you never know the depth of sorrow such as mine."

Lady Rosamond stood before her mirror to place a tiny rosebud in the raven hair that encircled her stately head in luxuriant coils. Slight and graceful in form, she saw indeed a pretty picture reflected there. It seemed to mock her with pitying gaze. Her black silk dress revealed the snowy whiteness of her beautifully rounded shoulders and arms, pure as the marble mantel upon which she rested. The costly locket, with its flashing diamonds, suspended by a heavy gold chain, rested upon her bosom. She thought of her father's kindness as she placed his gift to her lips, exclaiming, "Poor, dear papa, how I should like to see him to-night; I love him so fondly. If he knew what I am suffering perhaps he might relent. No doubt he is lonely to-night and wishing to see his 'only little girl,' as he lovingly calls me."

Presently Lady Rosamond was formally ushered into the apartment where the company, comprising the family and a few intimate friends, were assembled to divest the Christmas tree of its gay clothing and appendages.

As a veritable Santa Claus presented each present, the all-important Johnnie was ready to exclaim: "Thank old Sandy for that, can't you? What a hale old chap is Sandy!" Turning to Lieutenant Trevelyan, the incorrigible ventured to ask who might be Sandy's tailor?

When among the presents a tiny case, lined with white velvet, revealed a jewelled cross of exquisite design, Sir Howard exclaimed gaily, "Lady Rosamond, a coincidence--the cross followed by an anchor!" producing at the same time a costly ornament in the form of an anchor. "Have no fear, your cross is outweighed by the anchor Hope in the end. What a beautiful encouraging omen!"

CHAPTER VI.
ST. JOHN'S EVE.

It was St. John's Eve; Government House was a scene of splendour; truly every precinct was a blaze of dazzling light. Here was assembled the distinguished, gay, beauty, and wit of the Province; the learned and severe as well as the thoughtless. Hearts beat with throbbing and exciting pulsation, fired by hope's fondest dreams. The spacious drawing-room, already described in a preceding chapter, now assumed, if possible, a more brilliant aspect--flooded with light, rendered more effective by an additional chandelier, a gem of countless scintillations, distracting in variety and prismatic design. The courtly reception, high-born dignity and ease exhibited in every smile, gesture, word and action of the distinguished occupants, might recall vivid conceptions of the days when beauty and chivalry were conspicuous in homage to royalty and grand pageantry.

Amidst the pressure and arrival of each guest no confusion was apparent. Rank took precedence with studied regard. The many guests were attired in a style and elegance becoming the occasion. Conspicuous was the military rank of the large number of officers of His Majesty's service--colonels, majors, captains, lieutenants, ensigns, and all those insignias of like distinction. Among these might be found hidden, viscounts, lords, and baronets, and those aspiring to the proudest titles and birth of family. To describe the most imposing and costly dresses worn on this evening would be a difficult task. Ladies arrayed in the most gorgeous and priceless brocade and satins ablaze with diamonds and gems, snowy silks studded with pearls, velvet robes lined with costly furs and covered with lace at a fabulous price and texture, coronets of jewels, necklaces, bracelets, and beautiful trinkets, made the suggestion to a beholder that Heaven had showered down her radiation of delight by bestowing upon these jewels a reflection scarce less than that of her own upon the scene above. Among the throng none were more eagerly sought than Lady Rosamond; her quiet and easy dignity had won the regard and esteem of all those with whom she mingled. Unassuming and retiring, Lady Rosamond had excited no jealousy on the part of her less favored female friends. On her they all united in bestowing kind and sisterly regard. To gratify curiosity, and show our beautiful young friend as she appeared in the drawing-room, leaning on the arm of Captain Douglas, I will try describe her as nearly as possible:--A white satin robe with court train, bordered with the purest lace, festooned with pearls, over a blue satin petticoat, formed a lovely costume, with bodice of white satin, showing the faultless waist of the wearer; white satin slippers, ornamented with pearls, encased the tiny feet of Lady Rosamond. She was, indeed, worthy the name she bore--a type of her lovely but unfortunate ancestress, who won, for a time, the fickle heart of Henry Eighth, and gave birth to the good and pious young Edward.

Many smiles of recognition were bestowed upon the Lady Rosamond, among whom were those of the old cavaliers and statesmen, the middle-aged and the young and gay gallants of the day. If the latter showed any preference, as regards companionship, it was a strange preference for the more advanced in life. Ladies in the declining stage of life were to her the greatest source of comfort. To their varied experience of life the young girl would give the entire earnest of her truthful nature. Nor was this fact unnoticed. Lady Rosamond was the frequent partner of a revered grandfather, either at the whist table or in the quadrille, much to the secret annoyance of the young gentlemen present.

Mary Douglas was often at the side of her girl friend. It frequently happened that they were vis-a-vis in a quadrille, when Lady Rosamond indulged in exchanging playful sallies of mirthful character. In appearance, manners and companionship those lovely girls might be considered as sisters. On more than one occasion had such a mistake been of concurrence, while Mary Douglas was recognized as Lady Rosamond.

Colonel L----, an intimate friend of Sir Howard, remarked to a lady beside him, "This is truly an enjoyable affair. I am doubtful if many years hence some will not look back and say that this was one of the happiest moments of their life."

In the midst of this speech a gay and dashing young officer stepped forward, accosting a superior in command in a brotherly and familiar way, shewing behind a tie of relationship. Aside, in quiet tones, the younger exclaimed, "Cousin Charles, will you introduce me to the lady in crimson velvet and white satin, with tiara of diamonds?" "Certainly, Montague, whenever you wish. Do you not think her beautiful?" "Yes," was the reply, "but not in effect with Lady Rosamond or Miss Mary. Does not that lovely costume set off her ladyship's charms. How faultless her form! It is a hard matter to decide between the beauty of those companions."

This last remark caused a blush to suffuse the brow of a handsome youth standing within hearing. Suddenly turning away, and musing as he went, Lieutenant Trevelyan was half angry at himself for some slight betrayal of feeling which fortunately had not been detected.

As Lady Douglas was sitting in a corner, whither some of her guests had retired to rest from the fatigue of the evening, a lady near ventured to exclaim, "What a noble looking young man is Lieutenant Trevelyan! He has such a frank and honest face; besides, he is so kind and considerate. Having heard so many kind allusions towards him from so many sources, I have a great interest in his welfare. It is said that his father won distinction in the army."

"Yes," returned Lady Douglas, "I can remember his father when he really appeared not much older and wore the same blushing countenance as our dear friend Guy."

"Ah, there he is," exclaimed one of the eager admirers.

At this moment the subject of their remarks led forth Lady Rosamond as his partner in the dance.

"What a charming couple," said one. "How striking the contrast of their dress," said another, as the bright scarlet of Lieutenant Trevelyan's uniform reflected on the pure white satin of Lady Rosamond's bodice, while the blue satin added a pretty effect.

"How happy he looks as he smiles upon his partner," said one of the group.

"Who could be unhappy in the presence of Lady Rosamond?" replied Lady Douglas.

"Pardon, your ladyship, but there are many here who feel the hidden pain caused by one look or smile from her ladyship's lovely face." The speaker here lowered her voice, continuing: "I cannot explain or account for the feeling which prompts me, but I really think that Lieutenant Trevelyan is under the influence of those beautiful eyes, and really it would be the fondest of my dreams realized, having in both seen much to admire."

"Mrs. B----," said Lady Douglas, in playful tones of reproof. "You really would be tempted to become a match-maker?"

"Yes," replied the other, "if by any means I could further the present scheme."

"Lady Rosamond is indeed amiable and loveable, and worthy of a true and noble husband, while Lieutenant Trevelyan is in every sense a gentleman worthy the fairest and best. It would grieve me to see him rejected, yet, Lady Rosamond is not in a position to favor any suitor until she returns to England."

While the preceding remarks were being made by the group in the corner, the totally unconscious pair were apparently enjoying the music and dancing.

Lady Rosamond seemed in a sweet and uninterrupted dream of happiness, as she floated along in the mazes of the waltz, supported by the strong and graceful arms of her admirable partner, the young lieutenant. He likewise had his dreams, but of a different nature. He could not calmly enjoy the present in firm defiance of the future. A hopeless uncertainty lay before, which forbade approach. Lady Rosamond's reserve was a subject he dare not analyze. But the frankness which won him friends and passport had come to his relief just at the moment when his partner was most likely to chide with friendly courtesy. Both could look back to this evening during the course of after years.

When various amusements had succeeded, interspersed with dancing, the climax was yet to be reached. A grand surprise awaited. A tableaux was in preparation.

When the drawing-room was partially darkened the curtain rose, showing a simple background, with two children of the family sleeping quietly in the foreground. Standing over them was Helen Douglas; her hair fell over her shoulders. She wore a black dress, while a black lace veil, spangled with gold stars, covered her from head to foot. With her arms extended she is in the act of covering the sleeping children. A band of black, with silver crescent, on her forehead, and stars on the band, added to the beauty of the lovely Helen, and formed a true conception of the subject.

"Ah, the rogues," exclaimed Sir Howard; "how quietly they stole upon us."

Few failed to detect the word, showing a deep appreciation of the grace of Helen Douglas.

The second scene represented a parlor with a young girl in the foreground, having on her head an old-fashioned hood. This character is assumed by Arabella Farnham, the daughter of an officer retired from the service. Near the young lady stands a gentleman in the act of pulling off the hood to see her face. On the opposite side is another young girl in the person of Mary Douglas, in full evening dress, pointing to the hood, and laughing at its old and peculiar shape.

Much applause greeted the actors upon the success of these parts, but the crowning scene was the third and last--the united terms of the preceding ones. The effect was grand beyond description. The scene was supposed to be the great hall of Kenilworth, hung with silken tapestry, lit with numerous torches. The odor of choicest perfumes fell upon the senses, while soft strains of music floated in the distance. In the centre of the background forming this magnificent apartment was a chair of state, with canopy in imitation of a throne, and covered with rich drapery, on which is seated one personating Queen Elizabeth, whose smile is resting upon the courtly form of Walter Raleigh, upon whom she is in the act of conferring knighthood. Grouped around the throne are characters representing the Earls of Leicester, Essex, Oxford, Huntingdon, and a train of lords and ladies, conspicuous among whom was the Duchess of Rutland, the favorite maid of honor in Her Majesty's household. The character of Elizabeth was sustained by Lady Rosamond, arrayed in queenly robes and blazing with jewels.

"She looks every inch a queen," exclaimed one of the spectators.

"The young knight's heart is in a dangerous situation," said another.

"Beware, Sir Walter," said a third; "Essex and Leicester are dangerous rivals, especially the latter."

Kneeling with courtly grace was Lieutenant Trevelyan in the role of Sir Walter Raleigh. The young officer had performed his part with that graceful ease which had so won the affection of the great sovereign.

A slight shudder passed through the form of Lady Rosamond as she remembered his sad fate. Thinking the present no time for boding ill-starred events, she hastily turned her mind from the subject.

As the Earl of Leicester, Captain Douglas was apparelled in white. "His shoes were of white velvet, with white silk stockings, the upper part of white velvet lined with silver; his doublet, of cloth of silver; the close jerkin, of white velvet embroidered with silver and seed pearls; his girdle was of white velvet with buckles of gold. The scabbard of his sword was of white velvet and gold; his poniard and sword belt mounted with gold. Over he wore a loose robe of white satin with broad collar richly embroidered in gold. Around his neck was the golden collar of the garter, and around his knee the azure garter."[1] Truly was the costume executed, and raised admiration warm and long sustained.

Mr. Stanley, the son of an influential citizen, personated Sussex, who wore a purple velvet doublet, lined with golden cloth, and a richly embroidered jerkin of the same color with broad golden collar, black silk stockings and shoes of purple velvet. A richly ornamented girdle and gold mounted sword completed the costume, being rich and elegant and next in splendour to that of Leicester. The remaining nobles were dressed in courtly apparel and becoming the scene. Mary Douglas was, it is needless to add, in the capacity of the favorite Duchess of Rutland, the friend and confidante of Her Majesty. The whole had a beautiful effect and gave additional eclat to the evening's series of entertainments.

When Lady Rosamond again joined the dance, she was playfully advised to act well the policy of the character, by preserving towards the rival earls a well balanced line of judgment, and concealing any strong attachment toward the knight of the cloak, to Squire Lack-Cloak, as Raleigh was termed by the attendants at court.

Throughout the whole evening there was one who entered with heart and hand into the spirit of such gaiety--one foremost in the dance, foremost at the whist table, and foremost in gay and animating conversation. Notwithstanding those demands, there was another subject foremost in the mind of His Excellency's private secretary. Mr. Howe was a man of the world, gay, fascinating and striving to please. He had some faults, (and who has not?) but he had his good qualities full as well. He had a generous nature--a heart that wished well to his fellow man, and above all, his friends.

Since his arrival in New Brunswick, Mr. Howe had formed a strong attachment to his "boy friend," as he often designated the young lieutenant. Sir Howard was pleased with the fact and showed every encouragement by allowing Guy Trevelyan full privilege in his household. There were on several occasions within our notice, a troubled and half defined expression on the hitherto radiant and joyous counte-

---

1   Leicester's description taken from Sir Walter Scott.

nance of Guy Trevelyan. This fact had given much food for the mind of the secretary. After a scrutinizing search and untiring effort the hidden secret revealed itself in the bosom of Mr. Howe. He now possessed a *secret* that gave a *secret* pleasure by which the true nature of human sympathy could assert itself. Thus musing, and overjoyed at his recent success, Mr. Howe being reminded of the last dance, participated in the closing festivity celebrating St. John's Eve.

CHAPTER VII.
THE DISCLOSURE.

Winter had far advanced; its reign of severity and pitiless defiance was near its end. Already the genial days of joyous spring were heralded by a vigorous effort of the shrubs and plants to show themselves in resistance to the tyrannizing sway of the ice-crowned monarch. An occasional note from the returning songster was welcomed as the brightest harbinger of the truly delightful season. Merry voices mingled in tones of deep gratitude as they once more sallied forth to enjoy the pleasure of the woods.

None were more exultant than the inmates of Government House. From Sir Howard to the child at the feet of Lady Douglas, all shared alike in the pleasure of anticipation. Foremost in gleeful demonstration was the pioneer Johnnie, who danced and sang in the enjoyment of his native element--light and sunshine. Every hour that could be laid aside for this purpose was equal to a fortune.

But our young friend was no miser in this respect. Every available guest must be in readiness to join the incorrigible Johnnie when bent on his excursions. All stood on equal rights. Youth and age were all in the same order of classification. It was a remarkable trait of Johnnie's character that denials were not considered as sufficient excuse for delinquency on the part of any favored with invitations, and, in consequence, all made a point of being in readiness.

A bright Saturday morning had been arranged for one of those expeditions. April showers had already been the means of bringing forth flowers (if not May flowers), only to be found by the penetrating eyes of "Trapper Johnnie," as some of the more mischievous urchins had dared to designate their leader.

When, on the auspicious moment, at the marshalling of the clan, two had dared to break the rules, so strictly laid down, surprise was momentarily visible on many faces.

Lady Rosamond, the next in importance to Johnnie, had pleaded inability to attend, with a desire to retain her friend and companion. There was something in the pleading and beautiful eyes of Lady Rosamond that drove vexation at a respectful distance, and welcomed, in its stead, a feeling akin to sympathy within the heart of the manly boy. True chivalric dignity asserted itself in every form when necessity demanded. Her ladyship instantly received permission to remain, with a generous grace that made Johnnie a true hero in the estimation of his fair suppliant.

"Accept this favor, Sir Knight, as a token of the sincerity of your lady," said Lady Rosamond, stepping forward with a knot of pale blue silk in her hand.

With the brave gallantry of a Douglas, our hero knelt at the feet of her ladyship, and, receiving the favor, in graceful recognition kissed the fair hand that placed it there.

"Well done, my boy!" cried Sir Howard, who had been watching the ceremony from an open window, whence he had heard all that passed, and the circumstances which led to it; "you have already shown that spirit which I hope will always characterize my children."

After the picnickers had departed Lady Rosamond and Mary Douglas returned to the house, where they were met by Lady Douglas.

"My child, are you ill to-day?" said her ladyship; "you are unusually pale, while your eyes have a wearied look."

"I do not feel quite well this morning," returned Lady Rosamond, languidly.

"You need rest, my dear, after the fatigue of last evening; too much gaiety does not bring a bloom to my Rosamond," said her ladyship, kissing the pale cheek of the lovely girl, adding: "My dear, you must retire to your room, while I prepare a gentle sedative."

Lady Rosamond did retire. She also received the cooling draught from the fair hand of Lady Douglas, whose kindness shone in administering to the wants of others.

Poor Lady Rosamond's rest could not be gained by the simple sedative.

Physical ailments are not the worst form of suffering that afflict humanity. Lady Rosamond was enduring a mental conflict that was crushing in its intensity. The more she tried to baffle its power the more forcibly did it affect her. Vainly had she struggled within herself for aid, but no response. Faint hope dawned in the form of appeal. She now resolved to go to her dear companion with all her trials and tale of suffering. At intervals this hope died away, but in the end gained the mastery. It was this resolve that kept Lady Rosamond from joining in the festive train that set off that morning. It was this resolve that detained Mary Douglas as well. It was this resolve that bade Lady Rosamond to seek the quiet of her chamber preparatory to the trying disclosure.

Lady Douglas little divined the cause of those pale cheeks, as she ascribed them to the recent fatigue of an evening.

With heavy heart Lady Rosamond prepared for the reception of her confidante. A most beautiful picture is presented to the imagination in those lovely girls sitting side by side the arm of Mary Douglas around her companion.

"Mary, my love," began Lady Rosamond, "I have often longed for this moment, but could not summon the courage which the occasion demands."

"Rosamond, you startle me by your earnestness," said the former with deep surprise, dropping the title, as familiar companions, at the suggestion of her ladyship.

"Have patience, my darling; you shall hear it only too soon."

Between sighs and sobs Lady Rosamond told the whole history of her troubles--the letter and its stern proposal--not forgetting her father's kindness and his great love for her; "but oh!" she continued, "he cannot realize the depths of my misery."

"My poor darling," said Mary Douglas, with great tears dimming her beautiful eyes, "why did you thus suffer in silence? Can it be possible that you can have passed the long winter with such a weight upon your heart, my darling Rosamond?"

"Ah, my Mary," replied her ladyship, "I hope that you may never know how much the heart can bear, or how much woman, in her uncomplaining nature, may suffer. If I could only learn 'to suffer and be strong'--in that source lies my weakness. I am only one of the many thousands of my sex who have had such struggles. I do not wish to shirk the duty imposed on me, but if more strength were given me to bear it."

Mary Douglas sat in silence for some moments, as if waiting a sufficient reply. She knew her friend's disposition too well to venture any advice that would require a third person's knowledge of the matter. Gladly would she have referred it to her father or mother, but the idea gave no relief.

"Rosamond, my darling, if I could afford your mind instantaneous relief I would gladly do so, if even at a very great sacrifice. Of one thing rest assured--you have my service in any way that you wish to command me; besides, you have my sympathy and interest for life. It may be that I can slightly alleviate your sorrow. Can I not propose some plan in the future to re-arrange those affairs which at present seemed so irrevocably fixed? Kings have made laws to be broken when the cause demanded retribution. Darling, be more hopeful--trust in Providence and do the right--in the end you will be happy. Let me read your horoscope:--dark clouds within the visible horizon, succeeded by bright stars in ascension--hope and joy without fail."

A spirit of inspiration seemed to shine upon the face of Mary Douglas as she read her companion's future.

A smile lit up the features of Lady Rosamond.

"Thank heaven, darling, for that smile," said the gifted daughter of Sir Howard, throwing her arms around the sorrowing girl and kissing her affectionately.

Lady Rosamond felt happier and more encouraged from the fact of having such consolation and hope.

Mary Douglas had shed a ray of comfort in one unhappy heart. She knew not the load which was thus removed.

Lady Rosamond clung to those kind words with a fond pertinacity: not only the *words*, but the manner in which they were uttered.

Some evenings after the preceding interview had taken place, Sir Howard, Lady Douglas and family were assembled in the drawing room. Miss Douglas was seated at the piano, while Miss Mary Douglas sang the song so dear to every Scottish heart--Highland Mary. Lady Douglas listened to the melodies of her native land with heartfelt admiration. She loved to cultivate such taste on the part of her daughters. None could give a more perfect rendition of Scotch music and poetry than they.

When Miss Douglas sang "The Winter is Past," another of Burn's melodies, Mary Douglas fancied she saw the beautifully chiselled lips of Lady Rosamond tremulous with emotion. The first verse ran thus:

"The Winter is past, and the Summer's come at last,
And the little birds sing on every tree;

Now everything is glad, while I am very sad,
Since my true love is parted from me."

The finely cultivated voice of the singer entered fully into the spirit of the song, giving both expression and effect as she sang the last verse:

"All you that are in love and cannot it remove,
I pity the pains you endure:
For experience makes me know that your hearts are full of woe,
A woe that no mortal can cure."

"One would judge that my sister had some experience, if we take the face as an index of the mind," said Captain Douglas, in playful badinage directed towards his favorite sister, who in reality did have an experience, but not of her own.

She felt the blow thus unconsciously dealt at Lady Rosamond. Luckily for the latter, the coincidence thus passed over without any betrayal of feelings. In Mary Douglas was a firm and watchful ally. In her were reflected the feelings which passed unobserved in Lady Rosamond, or attributed to absence from home, separation from familiar faces, or clinging memories of the past. Another great source of protection lay in the composition of the character of the gifted ally.

Mary Douglas was possessed of a temperament most keenly sensitive to the finest perception of poetic feeling. Life to her was music and poetry. A beautiful picture either called forth joy or sorrow; a pathetic song thrilled her soul with well timed vibrations of feeling; a touching story brought tears to those lovely eyes, that would move one with pity. Thus was concealed the sympathy for Lady Rosamond, as none would sacrilegiously question those motives save in playful reminder from Captain Douglas, who bowed in fond adoration to the shrine of his sister's loveliness and goodness.

The entrance of Mr. Howe changed the current of conversation. Politics naturally took the lead. The House of Assembly being now three weeks in session, having opened April 15th, many important discussions took place. Much turmoil had to be suppressed by the sagacious judgment of Sir Howard. His predecessors had loudly contended against the troubles arising from the sources and expenditure of revenues. Happily, in the present administration, this matter had in a great measure subsided. For the general advancement of the Province, His Excellency left no means untried. His waking moments were almost entirely devoted to the interests of political welfare. His conversation within the family circle very often showed his zeal and the subject which lay near his heart. It was at this very time that he assembled all the legislators and influential citizens of Fredericton, addressing them in terms of burning eloquence, impressing on them the value of extending the progress of agriculture, showing the nature of the soil of New Brunswick; its perfect adaptation to the different kinds of products, and the independence of a country that can largely subsist upon its own resources. "The day will come, I hope," said Sir Howard, "when our farmers will be nobles of our land, and their sons and daughters ornaments to society, proud of the soil which raised them above the level of their less active fellow creatures."

As the speech had given rise to much comment throughout the different classes, it was freely discussed at Government House. This intelligent family often formed into a party of politicians and assumed the measured terms and knotty difficulties of political lore with an ease that was both instructive and amusing.

"If papa would favor this august assembly by taking the floor of the house, we might be more free to avow our feelings."

"I beg you will allow me to correct you, Miss Mary, as being rather sentimental in the choice of your last word," said Mr. Howe, appealing to Sir Howard with the question, "Your Excellency, have I not a right to make the correction?"

"I acknowledge your suggestion, Mr. Speaker," said Mary Douglas in her own defence, "and hope, before the session is over, to make a decided improvement both in views and technicalities."

"What!" exclaimed Captain Douglas, coming towards Mr. Howe. "Are you and Mary to take opposite measures already?"

"Not at all, sir," returned Mr. Howe, "I was merely setting her right on--" "technicalities," said the young girl, with a merry ringing laugh.

"Ah, Mary!" cried Charles Douglas, playfully pulling back the clustering ringlets from his sister's white forehead, "poetry and politics cannot exist on very intimate terms of friendship, at least too much poetry."

"Have a care, young man," said Sir Howard, laughing at the last remark.

"Ah! there are exceptions to every rule, sir, which you did not give me an opportunity to add, and I still make the former assertion to be, to a certain extent, counterbalanced by the latter."

From the appearance of different speakers the house seems to be out of order.

From playful remarks followed an interesting and varied stock of earnest political conversation, in which Lady Douglas joined with apparent ease. From agriculture the question led to education, one in which His Excellency had spent much time and labor.

It is to Sir Howard that the present university owes its first existence, its various stages of progress and final success. It was he who procured the first charter granting the privileges of a university. Few can realize the difficulties that Sir Howard met before accomplishing this great boon, and fewer still could see the way for raising the means necessary for the support of this institution. But an endowment was raised by grants from the revenue arising from the sale of unoccupied lands, and equal grants from the House of Assembly.

The next barrier presented by the colonists, for the suppression of the Thirty-nine Articles and the admission of Dissenters, was in itself a formidable array of difficulty, notwithstanding the next uprising of Episcopalian remonstrance. A sea of troubles! But reason, the true pilot, never deserted Sir Howard. The greatness of the cause was sufficient motive.

As the story progresses we hope to give a few facts which will prove what success awaited him. In the administration of this distinguished military ruler, New Brunswick found a warm and true-hearted friend and adviser--one whose memory is yet cherished within the hearts of those who had once seen his benignant and happy smile. Such is a faint picture of the domestic and political bearing of the gifted and distinguished Sir Howard.

CHAPTER VIII.
BEREFORD CASTLE.

In a beautifully remote district, between the celebrated towns of Hastings and Brighton, may be found the quaint old structure known as Bereford Castle. From the style of architecture it may be dated to the time of Edward the Third, bearing a striking resemblance to the castle re-erected in that monarch's reign by the Earl of Warwick. The castle of this period had degenerated or become more modernized. The closed fortress was rapidly assuming a mixture of the castle and mansion. Instead of the old Norman pile, with its two massive towers and arched gateway, thick walls, *oilets* and portcullis, Bereford Castle comprised stately and magnificent halls, banqueting rooms, galleries, and chambers. The keep was detached from the building, a stronghold in itself, surrounded by smaller towers and the important and necessary moat. During the civil wars it had stood many sieges, but, after repeated attacks, in the course of time it fell into decay. Much labor had been spent in repairing the part occupied as a residence until, at the present time, it was in good condition. The fine old park contained a valuable growth of trees--fir, spruce, pine, birch, elm, and the stately oak--which grew in luxuriant profusion. The north side of the castle commanded an extensive view of the surrounding hills, valley, and the winding river, with its numerous small inlets and tributaries.

The owners of Bereford Castle prided themselves upon their extensive gardens, for which purpose many obstructions had been removed. An artificial labyrinth of choice trees was contrived with marvellous effect, producing echoes of unceasing variety. In this enclosure, comprising many acres, were the most beautiful designs of parterres, borders, walks, galleries, cabinets, pavilions, porticoes, and many more intricate inventions of landscape gardening. Fountains gushed forth with untiring and fantastic wreaths of crystal foam; grottoes, cascades, mounts and precipices, seemed to steal away thought and quietly bear one to sleep to the music and dreams of fairyland.

The interior of the castle was in keeping with the grounds. The great hall which, in olden time, formed the most important part of the whole, was somewhat reduced in its dimensions. The windows of stained glass were emblazoned with the armorial bearings of the family, while the walls were adorned with life-size portraits of their ancestors. The richly carved roof, with its massive timbers and pillars supporting it; the old relics, in the shape of banners, helmets, swords, shields, and other implements of warfare, were arranged on every side. On each wing of the main building were spacious, modern rooms, occupied by the family as private apartments, viz: the drawing-room, dining-room, and sleeping apartments.

But perhaps the most attractive feature of the castle is the extensive library--an octagonal room in a small tower, apparently built at a recent date. The stained glass of its oriel window is very beautiful; the handsomely gilded ceiling and pannelled walls have a fine and striking effect; the floor is paved in marble, with inlaid mosaic; the shelves of rosewood and oak are filled with the most costly productions of literature, ancient and modern. This ancient family had cherished a fond taste for letters and science. The present lord, uncle of Lady Rosamond, still found leisure to devote many hours in his favorite resort--the library. Gerald Bereford cultivated a taste likewise. He was a young man of strong literary preferences, showing a desire for learning, with a keen appreciation of the pleasures and pastimes of daily life.

The drawing-room of Bereford Castle was indeed a superb display of taste, grace, wealth and classic design. Though firmly believing that a description will dispel the charm lingering around those beautiful rooms, I cannot resist the inclination to give one.

Lofty ceilings, frescoed and gilded, blazing in gold, with the arms of the family in bold relief; walls with wainscoting, arras and gorgeous tapestry. Furniture polished, carved and decorated; chairs embroidered in crimson and gold; Turkey carpets of fabulous price and texture; statuary, the work of ages; pictures, the work of a lifetime. Mediaeval grandeur in every niche and corner. Add to this a view of the gardens from the deep embayed windows, and you have a faint conception of the drawing-room scene at Bereford Castle, the intended home for Lady Rosamond Seymour.

Within this apartment are two occupants. Seated, or rather reclining, near the lower window is Maude Bereford, a young girl, graceful and intelligent, but possessing no claim to rare beauty. A second glance increases your approbation. Goodness of heart is indelible upon that face. The other occupant is a lady about sixty years of age. Time had been generous in its demands by drawing small usury from his allotted spoliations. Lady Bereford had been a beauty in her day, and, judging from the skilful devices practised, wished yet to retain her passing glories. Her fair complexion still showed a lingering bloom, the haughty eye still preserved a kindling glance, while her countenance and mien gave evidence of a stronger and more spirited cast of character than that of the young girl here mentioned.

"Maude," said her ladyship, "what news from Lady Rosamond?"

"Here is the letter, mamma, which you can read," said the young girl, at the same time placing a daintily folded letter in the lap of Lady Bereford.

With elevated eyebrows her ladyship looked over the contents of the letter. An occasional frown showed the displeasure which some sentences gave to the reader.

"It does not seem to please you, mamma," ventured Maude.

"I cannot think that Lady Rosamond is very complimentary to her friends in England. She makes no very kind allusions to her former companions here. You certainly will admit that fact."

"Oh, mamma, I am inclined to believe that you have formed mistaken opinions of dear Lady Rosamond. You see that she refers to scenes wherein all took a part, and I am sure that she is still my friend now as before she left us."

"Allow me, Maude," exclaimed Lady Bereford with impatient gesture, "you have neither age nor experience on your side; but I feel convinced that Rosamond has formed some attachment in New Brunswick, which she has cleverly concealed. Throughout her whole letter there is a want of earnestness that betrays her--an unsettled and vague uncertainty dictates every sentence. Sir Thomas did a very foolish action when he gave consent to his daughter's separation at a time when her nature is most susceptible to the temptations and flatteries of society."

"Mamma, I do not like to hear you speak thus of dear Rosamond. I love her dearly, and I could not bear the thought of her forming any attachment outside our family."

"That is one reason why I have been thinking so deeply upon the matter. That

Gerald loves his pretty cousin, we know full well, and the mortification of his being refused would be a heavy blow to our pride as well. From a conversation with Sir Thomas a few weeks ago, he gave us every assurance of an alliance of the families. Gerald is living on the consummation of his hopes being realized, while I would fain remind him of the line--'Hope deferred maketh the heart sick.'"

"Mamma, dear, you always seem to prefer the dark side," returned Maude. "Let us change the subject, as it is surely unjust to Rosamond."

"It is to be hoped that your fond dream may serve you aright," said her ladyship, with a tinge of sarcasm in her voice.

At that moment Maude Bereford arose and playfully approached the door wherein stood the future Lord Bereford, the heir of Bereford Castle.

Tall, handsome, and affable, Gerald Bereford bore a strong resemblance to her ladyship, but lacking that severity which predominated in the latter. Bold, regular features stamped the face of the young man. There was firmness about the mouth that indicated a strong energy and perseverance, at the sacrifice of much feeling. On the whole there was much in favor of Gerald Bereford's preferences; his clear, grey eye showed keen intellect, combined with mirth and humor; a deep manly voice, with purity of tone, spoke of truth and conscientious convictions. Such was the character and personal appearance of the nephew and favorite of Sir Thomas Seymour.

Maude led her brother to a seat beside Lady Bereford, and seated herself on a stool at his feet.

"Is this not a golden evening, Gerald?" questioned the young girl, looking up in her brother's face.

"Yes," replied Gerald, "but to enjoy the golden beauty, as you term it, I enforce strict and immediate attention to my wishes, and request your ladyship, and this little girl, will accept the escort of your liege lord."

"My liege lord will need those gallantries in reserve," returned the sister, in arch and naive tones.

Lady Bereford waived the imperative demand by desiring to remain. Maude accepted the proffered arm of Gerald to stroll beneath the inviting branches of the dear old oaks, so firmly interwoven in the scenes of innocent childhood and succeeding girlhood. The tender, sensitive girl loved her brother too deeply to believe that any could supplant his place in the love of Lady Rosamond. Her true criterion was the pure, innocent, and trusting love of a sister.

"Gerald, my dear, I am glad this opportunity has been so timely chosen," said the fond sister in an earnest tone, placing her delicate little hand upon her brother's shoulder.

"Pray, what has happened, Maude, that you look so sad?" said Gerald, breaking out into a hearty laugh.

"Nothing has happened," answered Maude; "really, if I look sad I do most wrongfully disavow my intention, having news for you--good news, too, I assure you," said Maude, again looking at her brother wistfully. "Can you not guess?" said she.

"How should I?" returned Gerald; "that would be a fruitless task."

"Since you have exercised such patience I will tell you," said Maude: "I have just received a letter from Rosamond."

A blush quickly overspread Gerald's face as he bowed acknowledgment.

Maude did not produce the letter which had been the cause of such annoyance to Lady Bereford, but she disclosed part of the contents and part she kept for herself. Together they talked long and earnestly. Though she took no liberty in showing the relationship in which she considered Lady Rosamond, her simple and earnest nature seemed to give assurance to Gerald. He listened to his sister's repeated praise of her companion--of their girlish attachment--and heartily hoped that Lady Rosamond would return the deep love which he had unreservedly placed at her disposal--his heart, name, riches--all were given the absent and beautiful maiden.

Musing awhile, Gerald was aroused by his sister, who almost petulantly exclaimed:

"Oh, Gerald, I do wish that Rosamond was home again, never to leave us. Two years separation seems a long time in the future. I grow so impatient. Do you know, Gerald," added Maude, with a bright eagerness, "I am going to write and urge her to shorten this lengthy probation. I cannot endure the thought. *Two years!*" repeated she, a second time, with strong emphasis.

"But you must remember the fable of the boys and the frogs," said Gerald, with an amused smile.

This remark reminded Maude of the sentiments of her mother, but she would not repeat them in the presence of her brother. She did not wish to cherish or countenance anything that would be disloyal to Lady Rosamond. In her sincerity she would not believe any views relating to her friend unless they received her direct sanction.

Gerald Bereford had misgivings regarding his hopes, but trusted that time and the favor of Sir Thomas would eventually disclose a brighter prospect. No jealousy had crossed his mind. Had Lady Bereford expressed her opinion in his presence he might have formed a far different view of the matter. At present all was tranquil. Maude's earnestness momentarily affected him--nothing more.

Lord Bereford, the present incumbent, was a man of sterling integrity--a firm friend of his brother-in-law, Sir Thomas Seymour. Though a man of high birth, distinguished, and sought by the great and learned, he was gentle, unassuming, and benign.

From her father Maude Bereford inherited the quiet and unobtrusive demeanor, so strongly in contrast to the haughty and obsequious bearing of Lady Bereford. Gerald was a strange compound of both--a fact that gave birth to the honest convictions of his nature.

Lord Bereford was an ardent admirer of Lady Rosamond--"a true Bereford,"-- the counterpart of her mother, Maria Bereford, whose beauty had been the theme of unusual admiration. For hours could he gaze upon his sister's child and recall the past, when a beautiful girl wandered through the old familiar spots and looked to him for brotherly sympathy when any annoyance rose before her. When the young girl grew to womanhood and gave her affection to his boyhood friend, Sir Thomas Seymour, he bestowed his blessing. Was he to repeat that blessing upon the child? Many times did Lord Bereford dwell upon this subject. His was a nature endowed with lasting qualities, true sympathy was the key note to his heart. He loved Lady Rosamond with devout, tender solicitude as his only daughter, and her happiness was his. If the love that Gerald Bereford bore towards his niece was not entirely reciprocated, and at the great sacrifice, would the true-hearted nobleman have urged upon Sir Thomas the error of his conduct? Such liberalism upon his part provoked the resentment of Lady Bereford, who could not brook any interference with the strictly defined principles of conservatism so long entailed upon every branch of her family. Sir Thomas Seymour was a staunch worshipper of his sister-in-law's doctrine. He cherished every idea with fondness, occasionally bringing them forth to view as opportunity favored. While Lady Rosamond is sadly watching the days and months drag slowly along within the bosom of Sir Howard Douglas' happy household, such are the motives actuating each of those who endeavor to seek her welfare; such is the state of their respective feelings, such their fond hope--their brightest dreams--laboring under the fatal delusion of giving happiness to her future.

Ah, your ladyship! were a kind fairy, in the form of a godmother, to breathe a few words into the ear of your loving and tender uncle, Lord Bereford, his kind heart would go forth to meet thee and save thee from a world of misery--from the fiery ordeal through which thou must pass!

CHAPTER IX.
MEMORABLE SCENES OF AUTUMN, 1825.

The summer and autumn of this year were indeed the most memorable in the annals of New Brunswick's history. Many there are still living who distinctly remember that awful visitation. The season of drought was unparalleled. Farmers looked aghast and trembled as they viewed the scanty, withered products of the land. All joined in the common uneasiness, daily awaiting relief. None felt more anxiety than Sir Howard Douglas, whose sole interests were those of his people.

Wishing to know the true state of the country, his Excellency made a tour of the farming districts, penetrating back settlements where the greatest suffering might be expected.

While absent on this errand of mercy, a sad misfortune befell the inmates of Government House. On the 19th of September their home was wrapped in devouring elements of flame, being almost entirely consumed.

It is on such occasions that the nobler side of our nature asserts its true dignity and shows qualities that otherwise would remain in obscurity. Lady Douglas, with calm and dignified composure, prepared her family to realize the situation, and with heroic firmness persisted in rescuing nearly all the valuables within Government House. The great assistance rendered by the citizens in their indefatigable labors, showed the unbounded and grateful respect borne towards this distinguished family. Every one was ready to offer aid. The daughters of Lady Douglas reflected her ladyship's cool intrepidity.

With tears in her eyes, Mary Douglas viewed the smoking mass where she had passed so many happy hours. Captain Charles Douglas, knowing well the tenor of his sister's poetic nature, kindly and encouragingly exclaimed, "Never mind, Mary dear; thank heaven no lives are lost. We will soon be united." Those simple words had the desired effect. The tender hearted maiden at once saw the ingratitude of her murmurs, and felt deeply thankful for her brother's gentle reproof.

Lady Rosamond, if possible, had stronger claims upon the heart of Mary Douglas and the entire household. She had wrought with a determination to do what she could--aye, more than she could. On being advised by Charles Douglas to desist, she firmly replied, "Not until everything is done that I can do."

A young officer, who happened to hear these words, received them as a valuable souvenir years afterwards, realizing their true worth.

It was, indeed, a most remarkable circumstance that so much valuable furniture and perishable articles were saved. One act of recklessness to be regretted was the cutting down of a valuable chandelier which, falling with a heavy crash, was shivered in a thousand pieces.

In a few days Lady Douglas and family sought shelter among their friends, from whom they received the strongest proofs of kindness. To a lady friend in England her ladyship writes: "The sympathy and real kindness received from the citizens of Fredericton I can never forget. The fire proved that the old adage, though homely, is a true one--'a friend in need is a friend indeed.'"

When Sir Howard returned, and was once more received in his family, he felt grateful to Providence for His kind deliverance. No vain or useless repinings marked the course of his conduct. With renewed energy this man of indomitable courage was again immersed in the public weal as well as the re-establishing of his family in comfortable quarters. A large and commodious building on King street, the property of Henry Smith, Esq.,[2] was now being prepared for the reception of His Excellency. The Government expended a considerable sum in making the necessary improvements, and within a very short time the citizens of Fredericton had the pleasure of seeing their beloved ruler and his family once more situated in a happy home. But Sir Howard was to face more terrific and threatening dangers. His unbounded sympathies had further and unlimited room for exercise.

October came, attended by the long continued drought. Gloom was depicted on every side. Many conjectures were afloat regarding the vicinity of the fire, which gave evidence of its existence in the density of smoke that filled the atmosphere.

---

2   The house at present occupied by Chief Justice Allen.

In the midst of this impending danger, on the 7th October, a fire broke out in the woods surrounding "The Hermitage," the residence of the Hon. Thomas Baillie, on the Government House road. Here the forethought of Sir Howard was exhibited with unequalled prudence, having every available engine and means of succor close at hand. By great exertions the house was saved. Danger still lurked in the woods. Within an hour an alarm was given in the city. Sir Howard was the first on the spot, having ridden furiously his spirited and favorite steed. Engines were again in quick action, while the military were only a short distance behind, being ordered up at the double.

The scene was terrific. High winds blew the fire from one building to the next, until the third part of the city was a mountain of flame--cracking, roaring, tremendous in its fury. Water was kept up in constant streams, having but little effect. Many sat down and cried in their frantic emotion. Hundreds of families without home, food, or clothing.

In the midst of this sickening sight was one whose very presence lifted a weight from the hearts of the sad and homeless. Sir Howard never once deserted his post--working, encouraging, and aiding. By his advice the fire was stayed--two-thirds of the town still remaining. The stifling air and glowing heavens made the hearts of many grow sick and faint.

Perhaps it would be wiser to end the tale of misery here, but as the chapter would seem incomplete, it may be necessary to make slight allusion to a wilder and more terrible fire.

The consummation of terror, madness, and dismay, depicted in its most awful form, would fail to do justice to this sickening calamity--the Miramichi fire.

The forests, for hundreds of miles in every direction, were one solid mass of living fire, roaring louder than thunder; in its fury shaking the bowels of the earth and leaping up to the heavens which seemed, also, to be enveloped in flames. Nothing more awful will be witnessed until the judgment day. Many were of opinion that the time was at hand when "the heavens and earth shall melt away." Hundreds lost their lives, while property was destroyed to an immense amount.

An ordinary mind would have sunk under the weight of grievances that pressed on all sides; but Sir Howard Douglas rose above the situation. With Spartan firmness and unswerving courage he set about raising means for the distressed by subscription, both at home and abroad, in money, food, and clothing. Letters were sent to all parts of America, England, and Ireland. Not thus content, Sir Howard went himself to visit burnt districts where man or beast could scarcely penetrate, climbing over miles of fallen brushwood. Those poor creatures tried to show their gratitude by words, but were unable. Their tears were a more gracious tribute than jewels--being the grateful offering of a stricken community. Their benefactor had conveyed provision for their sustenance, and clothing for their wives and families. Many were the fervent prayers offered for their noble-hearted and humane ruler, and none more gratefully acknowledged these than he.

Much more might be told in connection with those sad events, but as the details might not be acceptable to the reader, therefore we refrain.

Once more gathered in their home, the family of Sir Howard were not inactive. The spirit of charity was manifest in every action of those lovely girls. Mary Douglas and Lady Rosamond had formed a sewing circle, to which they invited some of their young acquaintances. In this charitable employment they spent many hours. Clothing was made and distributed with increasing demand. The severity of winter caused many poor people to look for assistance in every possible form. Gaiety was for a time forgotten. Festive parties and sumptuous array were set aside for the necessities of the season.

It is a well established fact that the miseries of others often alleviate our own. To none could this application be more forcible than Lady Rosamond. In her bitterness of heart she experienced a quiet relief in assisting her companions to provide clothing for the sufferers. The scenes through which she had passed counterbalanced the feelings she had hitherto experienced and taught her gentle resignation. Her thoughts were of a more serious nature--a source whence she derived much comfort. Her parent's views were unaltered; her hopes were no brighter in the distant future, but, as afterwards expressed, she had more strength given her from the bitter trials of suffering humanity.

As Christmas drew nigh the inmates of Government House could not resist a desire to look back to the joyous season which they had passed in the home now laid low, its surrounding woods, their pleasant excursions, and the extensive preparations in decorating for the festive scenes that followed.

Pioneer Johnnie was loud in regrets for the apparent neglect which the sylvan deities must naturally feel by his temporary absence from their select and stately assemblages.

"Keep up your spirits, Master Johnnie," once remarked Lady Rosamond, "the next time we go back the trees will recognize the compliment with music and grateful homage."

"As none but you and Lady Rosamond regret being turned out, I presume," exclaimed Charles Douglas, who was always ready to join any conversation that afforded amusement. He continued passing careless jokes until the clock in the hall reminded him of his business.

"Really, Lady Rosamond, I credit you with driving away dull care and my forfeiting all claims to the future good will of my friend Howe by disregarding his message. Pardon me, ladies, for having almost forgotten to say that the sleigh will be in readiness in half an hour."

"Half an hour," exclaimed Mary Douglas, somewhat hastily, "really, Charles, I cannot pardon you for such neglect, as it sadly interferes with my plans."

"Come, little one, frowns do not become thy brow," returned Captain Douglas, kissing the forehead of his sister.

"That is much prettier," said he, pointing to the smiling face which in turn rested upon him.

Taking up a book which lay open beside the seat hitherto occupied by Lady Rosamond, Captain Douglas commenced to read some lines from Tennyson, when accosted by his companion, Mr. Howe:

"You seem to be taking things very cool, old fellow. Where are the ladies?"

"They are getting ready; come in while we are waiting."

"This is your fault again, Douglas. It is past the hour, and a large party awaits us," said Mr. Howe impatiently.

"Better late than never," vociferated Captain Douglas, as he went out singing, quickly returning with Mary Douglas and Lady Rosamond.

"It is all Charles' fault," said the former, by way of explanation.

"Ha, ha, ha," laughed Captain Douglas, "I knew this was coming, but I must be as jolly as I can."

"Your ladyship is under my protection," said the incorrigible delinquent, offering his arm to Lady Rosamond, while Mary Douglas was assigned to the companionship of the private secretary.

"This is indeed a merry party," said Lady Rosamond to her gallant, as he placed her beside him and wrapped the daintily lined robes around her.

"I am half inclined to be angry with Trevelyan," said Mr. Howe, turning around in his seat and facing Captain Douglas.

"What are your grounds?" questioned the latter.

"Enough to justify my declaration," said the former, apparently looking at Captain Douglas, but in reality casting sidelong glances at Lady Rosamond.

What did he seek there? Did jealousy cause that stolen glance? What was the motive? These important questions certainly deserve some attention, which, in justice to Mr. Howe and the parties concerned, and last, but not least, the reader, this concession must be granted.

As admitted, the private secretary of Sir Howard Douglas entertained a warm friendship towards Lieutenant Trevelyan, treating him with the tenderness of a younger brother. Being constantly thrown in the society of each other, there was much to be learned on both sides. That the young lieutenant returned this friendship he took no pains to conceal, knowing that in Mr. Howe he had an interested friend and adviser. For some time in the past the keen eye of the former detected a sudden strange and half concealed manner possessing his young friend, which completely puzzled him: Various conjectures presented themselves, but all unsatisfactory and vague. Still further watch was kept upon the actions of Guy Trevelyan, but nothing appeared to solve the difficult problem. An opportunity at last rewarded this perseverance. As explained in a preceding chapter, one side of mysterious question was solved without any effort or seeking the on the part of any one. By a mere accident Mr. Howe learned the cause which had so deeply influenced the course of Guy Trevelyan's actions, and, furthermore, his feelings. Here was something gained: did it bode good or evil to the young lieutenant?

These were questions that revolved themselves in the mind of the reasoner. Gladly would he do anything that would further the interest of his young friend, yet there might be a likelihood of stretching this prerogative if it in anywise interfered with the direct affairs of another. Whichever view of the matter was taken difficulty arose on every hand.

Let us hasten to the main point of the argument. That Lieutenant Trevelyan loved Lady Rosamond with a pure and ardent love was a matter beyond doubt. She was the ruling passion that influenced every action, guarded or unguarded. It was this knowledge that now gave the secretary so much perplexity. He entertained towards Lady Rosamond a kind and friendly regard; he was willing to serve her under any ordinary circumstances and in any friendly capacity. In the present instance Lady Rosamond was under the charge and protection of Lady Douglas, who would be, in a measure, responsible for any attachment thus formed while she remained her guest. On this point were many conscientious scruples to be overcome, which did not meet the approval of that course of honor which had hitherto characterized Mr. Howe's principles and actions. He must not sacrifice these even at the great risk of gaining the happiness of a young and respected friend.

But the sight of the young lieutenant pleaded more eloquently than the most glowing and pathetic language. His thoughtful eyes, his pure white forehead, and clustering ringlets of chestnut hair, had a wealth of appeal hidden beneath, conveying more subtle beauty than the production of the countless volumes of mystic ages. Thus situated, the secretary felt the awkwardness of his position. It was not curiosity that prompted; it was a secret influence which the young lieutenant inspired--an influence that held the former bound and enchained with no means of escape at hand.

CHAPTER X.
THE INTERVIEW.

I n a small but handsome reception room adjoining the library of Bereford Castle sat its stately mistress, with an impatient and eager look upon her countenance. Trifling with a pretty trinket which she has in her hand, her ladyship
is apparently ill at ease. Something has given cause for annoyance and grave
deliberation. An anxious and hasty glance towards the door, shows that a visitor is
momentarily awaited.

Taking advantage of these moments, I will occupy them in dilating upon a few
of the qualities and characteristics of the distinguished occupant. Lady Bereford was
a woman of shrewdness and capacity, possessing a subtle weight of influence that
bore with irresistible force, and was stoutly prepared to resist an opposing element
in any quarter. The daughter of a London barrister of considerable reputation, her
ladyship dwelt with pride upon her fond preference for the legal profession. Her
conversation was frequently interspersed with learned remarks, savoring of the in-
ner temple, its dingy courts, volumes of dust and musty manuscripts. "Evidence and
proof" were leading points always at hand. Caution was the inevitable watchword,
based upon a scrutinizing and at times heartless penetration. In short, the character
of Lady Bereford might be summed up in a few words--as a cool, clever and calculating woman of the world--one not to be baffled by ordinary circumstances. On
the present occasion her eye has a fire in its depths that brooks no interference. Her
brows are knotted with an angry frown; as she raises them hastily, the frown has
departed. The small and still plump white hand is extended. Sir Thomas Seymour
bows very low, receives the hand, kissing the tips of the taper fingers, is seated in an
elegantly embroidered fauteuil opposite her ladyship.

After the usual pleasantries had passed, Sir Thomas commenced by way of explanation:

"Your ladyship will pardon this detention, from the fact of my being absent when your note arrived. Business demanding my presence at the admiralty office I was unavoidably detained for some days. On arriving yesterday I immediately telegraphed the fact to Lord Bereford, but hope that the present misfortune will not seriously interfere with any of your ladyship's plans."

Assuming an air of much importance, her ladyship began; "When I addressed you, it was merely in the form of a note, not wishing to convey a subject of such importance to paper, deeming that it demanded your personal attention. I fully exonerate you by the ready response as shown at this instance."

This remark Sir Thomas politely acknowledged with a deep bow, while a shade of uneasiness was visible upon his features.

With another assuming air to gain, if possible, a more wise and legal manner, her ladyship thus resumed: "Sir Thomas, you must certainly be aware of my motives in thus requesting an interview. You cannot be insensible to the fact that it entirely concerns the Lady Rosamond."

Here Sir Thomas became somewhat agitated, but her ladyship continued: "Strictly speaking, it concerns both families, as how can it apply to the former without a direct application to Gerald Bereford, in which case is involved that of his connexions."

Sir Thomas felt the necessity of waiving those points of nicety, but knowing too well that any interference would entail a more definite investigation, listened with utmost composure in the hope of instant relief.

With the stem gravity of a learned judge, ready to pronounce sentence upon the culprit arraigned, her ladyship in graver tone continued: "I cannot but admit that the matter has given me very great annoyance. I again refer to Lady Rosamond."

The affair, at each mention of the latter, assumed a graver importance, while Sir Thomas inwardly struggled to maintain a studied demeanor as becoming the grave occasion.

"You are possibly not aware of the position in which her ladyship is being placed by this temporary separation from her family?" ventured Lady Bereford, with full interrogative force that at length afforded an opportunity to Sir Thomas.

"The matter," returned he, "has never given me any serious apprehensions, and, pardon me, I must confess to your ladyship that there seem no apparent grounds for any. Lady Rosamond has been made acquainted with our views regarding Gerald, and knowing this, I have too much confidence in her nature to harbor a thought that she will either, in word or action, entertain a wish in opposition to that of a fond and solicitous parent."

"I admit that Lady Rosamond is indeed a worthy and dutiful daughter; yet, pardon me, there are many little undesirable and inconsistent fancies which, in the waywardness of youth, are ready to take form in the tender and susceptible nature of a young girl, and which, if not constantly watched, assume a degree of strength almost uncontrollable. Allow me to state the case," continued her ladyship, "when, perhaps, you may see the matter in a clearer light."

At mention of the word *case* Sir Thomas dreaded another succession of legal points, but demurely listened to the following version:

"You have unwittingly placed your child in a very dangerous position. To none would I so readily give the protection of my daughter as Lady Douglas, who is, in every sense, a true mother and a dignified woman; yet there are moments when Lady Rosamond can assert her right to control her own impulses and feelings. As a guest she has an entire right, while it would otherwise be a stretch of prerogative on the part of the guardian."

"You cannot but admit," said her ladyship, still bent on influencing her attentive listener, "that Lady Rosamond is indeed very beautiful, which alone has sufficient reason to sustain my argument. Beauty, through countless ages, has been the source of much misery. Through Helen was lost a Troy; Cleopatra, Roman glory."

Her ladyship was going to cite further examples when interrupted by Sir Thomas exclaiming:

"Your ladyship will pardon me, but it would certainly be deep injustice at present to raise an objection on this point; it surely did not bring misery in its train to Lord Bereford."

At this compliment to her beauty and vanity, a rare smile lit the face of Lady Bereford, while she gaily added:

"Sir Thomas, you still cling to your former gallantry with the pertinacity of an ill-favored suitor."

Seeing that the last evidence was ill-grounded, her ladyship, having reconsidered the situation, again resumed:

"You must admit that among the military staff of Sir Howard Douglas there are many attractive and eligible young gentlemen worthy of the hand of the fairest. Besides, there are many families holding high position in New Brunswick, the descendants of persons of rank equal to our own. Among these are gentlemen--brave, handsome, and equally fascinating. It would indeed be a very extraordinary case if the Lady Rosamond, with all her beauty and accomplishments, daily surrounded by an admiring crowd, should not unconsciously fall a prey to her already susceptible nature. Sir Thomas," continued her ladyship, with more vehemence in her manner, "you do not seem to weigh matters as I do, or you would certainly see the error you have committed--the great wrong you have done to your child. Were I to disclose the facts, they would astonish you, but if in the future, when too late you make such a discovery, you will have only yourself to blame. That Lady Rosamond has formed an attachment I am certain; of its value I am not prepared to say; but, in honor to Gerald Bereford, I have a right to demand your attention."

At this sudden declaration Sir Thomas was astounded.

"Where is the proof of this?" demanded he in startling surprise.

Her ladyship then referred to the letter--its unconnected and half-hidden sentences--and expressed her firm conviction of the certainty of those predictions.

Sir Thomas drew a sigh of relief when he found no stronger evidence against the straightforward and conscientious spirit that had hitherto pervaded his loved child.

Lady Bereford possessed the tactics of a clever reasoner. When she had failed in bringing her own arguments to bear directly she had recourse to more forcible measures. The mention of Gerald Bereford had instantaneous effect. Sir Thomas' eye brightened with renewed lustre; his whole expression betrayed the ruling passion within him. Her ladyship took advantage of the situation.

"If you will empower me to act in this case there will be no further trouble to be apprehended. Woman is the best judge of woman. Leave the matter in my hands, Sir Thomas, and you will have no further anxiety. I will assure you that Gerald will meet no refusal when he asks Lady Rosamond to become his wife."

Sir Thomas yielded. He knew that in this lay his child's happiness, which, as a parent, he was in duty bound to promote.

"Your ladyship is right," exclaimed Sir Thomas, "but in granting this I request that you will not in any way shorten the visit of Lady Rosamond."

"Rest assured," cried her ladyship, "that no such demands will be made. The happiness of her ladyship will be our sole interest; kind and friendly advice, with gentle admonition, is the only safeguard."

When Lady Bereford had gained the case (according to her legal version) her manner changed as if by magic. Gay smiles played over her features with inexpressible delight; her voice was soft, smooth, and bewitching with sweetness.

Sir Thomas was persuaded to remain to luncheon. The party consisted of the family, Sir Thomas, and Colonel Trevelyan, a gentleman whose acquaintance Lord Bereford formed while visiting an old friend. The conversation was friendly and animated. Many topics of general interest afforded them an opportunity to pass the hours in a pleasant, lively and genial manner. Having by accident referred to his connection with the Peninsula campaign, Lord Bereford was delighted to find another intimate friend of Sir Howard Douglas. Sir Thomas Seymour joined heartily in the general discourse. Colonel Trevelyan, or properly speaking Sir Guy Trevelyan, told many incidents of military and social life, in which Sir Howard and himself had figured quite conspicuously.

Great was Maude Bereford's delight when she learned that the young officer, so often alluded to in the letters received from Mary Douglas, was the son of their guest. At this intelligence a sudden frown rested on Lady Bereford's brow, but momentarily vanished. She had gained her point; such matters did not so forcibly affect her now. Naturally many inquiries were made respecting the young lieutenant, all of which were answered in a quiet and unassuming way. The character of the father betrayed that of his son. Without questioning why Maude Bereford felt a deep interest in the young unknown, she had already been forming plans of inquiry to ascertain a further knowledge. Lady Rosamond would certainly be able to give her a correct description. Certainly her ladyship must spend much time in the company of one who had such claims on the friendship of Sir Howard. Reasoning thus was the gentle daughter of Lady Bereford, while the latter was exultant in having formed a plan for the furtherance of a scheme which lay near her heart.

The next morning her ladyship was alone in her boudoir. A delicately folded sheet lay upon the exquisitely inlaid writing desk before her. Satisfaction beams upon her by occasional smiles. Again she seizes the unclosed letter, examines closely its contents, and, with evident ease, places it in an envelope which she seals and addresses. A servant in livery answers the summons of a silver bell standing beside the desk. Her ladyship, drawing aside a hanging of silver tissue, approaches the door where the missive is delivered in charge of the liveried attendant. With a sense of relief Lady Bereford returns to the library to await the morning mail.

Lady Bereford indeed lavished all the fondness of a mother's pride upon her first-born. Maude was to her a simple-minded, gentle girl, whose sole influence was her mother's will. The daughter of Lord Bereford was a true type of her father: gentle, conscientious and sympathetic.

In Lady Rosamond, Maude Bereford could see no reason for such anxiety as was manifested by her mother, yet she would feel disappointed if her companion would form another attachment. Maude loved her brother with all the tenderness of her nature, while Gerald Bereford returned this love with deep fervent gratitude. His sister was to him the connecting link with Lady Rosamond. He took pleasure in daily walks with Maude, whose playful childish ways often reminded him of the absent cousin. The future lord of Bereford Castle was worthy the love of the fairest, purest and truest. He possessed a spirit of independent manliness, and would brook no favor that was not warranted by honor.

When Gerald Bereford asked his uncle for a right to address the Lady Rosamond, it was from a spirit of honor. He dearly loved the beautiful girl, though he had never avowed his feelings, and when she treated his advances with coolness, he still cherished the hope that in the end his love would be reciprocated. On receiving the joyful assurance from Sir Thomas that the great object of both families was the consummation of these hopes, the ardent lover was happy beyond doubt. Sir Thomas had led Gerald Bereford to believe that the Lady Rosamond had always favoured his suit, but in girlish caprice had refused him any encouragement until the expiration of her visit, when she would return home ready to receive the courtly attentions of her relative.

Cheered by these fond assurances, Gerald Bereford did anxiously look forward to Lady Rosamond's return. Sir Thomas had indeed communicated this matter to his nephew with a firm assurance of the realization on the part of both. He doubted the true feelings of his child, but he was determined that the event should take place after sufficient time had elapsed. Lady Bereford knew that Sir Thomas was really deceiving himself as well as his nephew; but with the keen perception of her nature, kept her own counsel. She, as well as Sir Thomas, was determined to carry out her design, for which purpose she closely concealed part of her views from Maude upon the reading of Lady Rosamond's letter, also her message to Sir Thomas, their interview, concessions and result.

Practical and calculating woman of the world as was Lady Bereford, might it be possible that she could heartlessly seal that daintily perfumed missive which was to become the source of such almost unendurable anguish? Really, one would fain exculpate her ladyship of the great wrong--a wrong which for years could not be obliterated from the hearts of those whose sufferings were borne silently and without reproach, each bearing the burden with a sickening heart, feeling that death would be a happy relief.

What a world is ours. What a problem is life. Is there any word in the English language more suggestive? Life--its surroundings, aspects, all its outward associations. Is this the limit? Would to Heaven in some instances it were so, that the end be thus. What a hollow mockery does it impart to the heart of Lady Rosamond, whose cause of misery remains as yet half told. Life--a troubled dream, a waking reality, yet we cling to it with fond delusive hopes. What astute reasoner will solve, the intricacies of this problem? Can one who has suffered? The muffled throes of crushed hearts are the only response. God pity them!

CHAPTER XI.
FREDERICTON: ITS BUILDINGS, PUBLIC HOUSES, AMUSEMENTS, ETC

The year following the great fire was marked by great progress throughout the Province. Farmers were again in homes which they had built upon the site of those destroyed by the devouring element. Fields once more showed signs of cultivation. With Sir Howard Douglas to stimulate the prosperity of his people, progress was the watchword--the general impulse.

Fredericton, like the phoenix, had arisen from its ashes; buildings arose in rapid succession. Wooden houses of moderate pretensions lined Queen and King streets, from Westmorland to Carleton street, the limit of the burnt district.

Business was carried on by a few upright and enterprising merchants, foremost of whom stood Rankine & Co., the leading firm of the city. This establishment was situated on Queen street, between Northumberland and Westmorland streets, in which was constantly pouring an unlimited source of supplies for conducting the immense lumber trade established by this firm, whose name shall be remembered while New Brunswick shall continue to produce one stick of timber. Many farmers of that time yet have occasion to refer to the generosity which characterized this long established firm. Many yet bless the name of Rankine & Co.

The public buildings of our city were in keeping with the private residences. No Barker House or Queen Hotel adorned our principal street as now; no City Hall, Normal School, or Court House. On the present site of the Barker House was a long two-story wooden building, designated as Hooper's Hotel under the proprietorship of Mr. Hooper. This was the only accommodation for public dinners, large parties, balls, etc In this hotel the St. George Society annually celebrated their anniversary by a grand dinner party where heart-stirring speeches, toasts and patriotic songs, were the general order of programme, of which the following verses are an example. They were composed in April 1828, and sung by one of the members of this society at a public dinner that year, after the toast of "Lord Aylmer and the Colonies." The idea was suggested to the young law student by looking upon a map showing the territory explored by the Cabots and called Cabotia. The writer will be readily recognized as one of New Brunswick's most eloquent, gifted, and favored statesmen, recently holding the highest position in the Province:--

When England bright,
With Freedom's light,
Shone forth in dazzling splendor,
She scorned to hold,
The more than gold,
From those who did befriend her;
At space she spurned,
With love she burned,
And straight across the ocean
Sent Freedom's rays,
T' illume their days
And quell their sons' commotion.
Hail, Britannia!
Thou loving, kind Britannia!
Ne'er failed to wield
Thy spear and shield.
To guard our soil, Britannia!

But rebels choose
For to refuse,
The boon thus kindly granted,
And with vile art,
In many a heart,
Black discord's seeds they planted;

Now civil war,
In bloody car,
Rode forth--and Desolation,
Extended wide,
Its horrid stride
For mock emancipation.
O Cabotia!
Old England's child Cabotia!
No rebel cloud[3]
Did e'er enshroud
Thy sacred soil, Cabotia!

The purple flood
Of traitors' blood
Sent vapors black to heaven,
And hid the blaze
Of Freedom's rays,
By a kind parent given;
But Liberty,
Quite loath to see,
America neglected,
Came to our land,
And with kind hand
Her temple here erected;
O Cabotia!
Them favored land, Cabotia!
While we have breath
We'll smile at death,
To guard thy soil, Cabotia!

When foreign foes
We did oppose,

---

3   Long before the Canadian Rebellion.

Britannia stood our second,
And those we fought
Were dearly taught,
Without their host they reckoned;
And should they now,
With hostile prow,
But press, our lakes and rivers,
The Giant-stroke,
From British oak,
Would rend their keels to shivers.
And thou, Cabotia!
Old England's child Cabotia!
Would see thy race
In death's embrace
Before they'd yield Cabotia!

While Shamrock, Rose,
And Thistle grow,
So close together blended,
New Brunswick ne'er
Will need to fear,
But that she'll be befriended;
We need not quake,
For nought can break
The sacred ties that bind us,
And those, who'd spoil
Our hallowed soil,
True blue are sure to find us.
O Cabotia!
Our native land, Cabotia!
For thee we'll drain
Our every vein,
Old England's Child Cabotia!

Here the St. Andrews Society also gave their national celebration. Last, but not least, came the St. Patrick Society. The last named might, indeed, be called ***the*** Society. Aided and encouraged by Colonel Minchin, Hon. Thomas Bailie, Mr. Phair, and many other distinguished Irish gentlemen, the St. Patrick's Society of Fredericton at that time attained a high social position. On St. Patrick's eve a yearly celebration also took place, the place of rendezvous being situated on Carleton street, adjoining the building now occupied as the post office. Eloquent and patriotic speeches were the leading features of those meetings. The following instance will serve to give an idea of the spirit which inspired those reunions. On one occasion a member of this organization--a well-known citizen of Fredericton for many years--spoke as follows: "Mr. President and gentlemen, I wish to call your attention to a subject which should fire the heart of every Irishman. Who was the gallant soldier, the true patriot, the hero who never once shrank from the fiercest of the fight, whose only glory was in his country's cause? Who led his army conquering and to conquer, facing the foe with the calm and intrepid coolness of one who knew not the meaning of fear? Who fought with fierce determination to conquer or die when surrounded by thousands of armed guerillas on the outskirts of Spain? Who dared to face Napoleon? Who dared to conquer the iron will of the Bourbon mandate? Who but the proud 'hero of a hundred fights,'--the Duke of Wellington! What country gave him birth?" "Ireland!" was the answer, amid deafening shouts of applause which caused the building to shake beneath their feet. This is but one of the stories told of those meetings, showing the spirit of interest manifested.

To return to hotels. On the site at present occupied by the Queen Hotel formerly stood the Market Inn, kept by Mr. Richard Staples. This was a comfortable and convenient house, frequented by farmers as they came to the city to dispose of their produce. In those days people settled principally near the St. John river and its numerous tributaries, with their lakes; therefore farmers generally used small boats for means of conveyance, waggons being looked upon as an extravagant luxury. Another public house, kept by Mr. Robert Welch, and known as the Albion Hotel, also occupied a prominent position, being well furnished and affording comfort and good accommodation to the travelling public. On Waterloo Row was situated the time-honored Royal Oak, kept by Miss Polly Van Horn, a name well known to those residing in the lower country districts.

Of other public institutions less may be said. On the square now adorned by the imposing City Hall, with its memorable clock, formerly stood or rather squatted the old Tank House, serving rather in the capacity of use than ornament. An old marketplace occupied the ground on which is now erected the County Court House.

It would be impossible to enter into details regarding every building; we merely cite a few facts to give a general idea of the situation of Fredericton at that time.

Before leaving these matters we must not omit mention of a quiet social organization then known as the Philharmonic Society. It was composed of a number of young gentlemen, members of the most influential families of the city. Wallace, band-master of H. M. 52nd regiment, took an active part in instructing these youths, who, within a short period, had acquired such proficiency as to enable them to give a series of entertainments in Hooper's Hotel. These consisted of selections displaying musical skill, ability and taste.

Conspicuous among the members of the Philharmonic Society was a young student named Vivian Yorke, afterwards a member of the legal profession; in later years, his burning eloquence had power to thrill the eager audience attendant upon his appearance. As a lover of music, the young scholar had from his childhood won a reputation beyond his years, while his association with the organization had given it a stimulus worthy such encouragement. Vivian Yorke had won high position within the social circle as well. His genial disposition, frank, manly bearing, dignified form and handsome face were sufficient passports irrespective of his other claims to distinction. It is almost needless to add, that Mr. Yorke stood high in the estimation of the band-master, who arranged several airs especially adapted to a number of patriotic songs composed by his talented pupil. In succeeding chapters we will allude to the rising career of Mr. Yorke as the occasion demands.

In this year the House of Assembly was opened by a warm debate upon the College Bill, which received stout resistance from all dissenting bodies. The episcopalians sought aid from the Archbishop of Canterbury and the Bishop of Nova Scotia. But the judgment of Sir Howard was equal to the occasion. His measures were such as must ultimately accomplish the desired end.

The 52nd Regiment, as yet stationed in Fredericton, still maintained their unbounded popularity, entertained their many friends at princely dinners, gave an unlimited number of balls, parties and festive gatherings. The race course still continued to be the daily resort for the distinguished horsemen. Races were a favorite pastime. Cricket and foot-ball had now become quite common. On the old square situated between York street and Wilmot's alley the youths of the city daily assembled to practise these sports, while the military occupied a space within their own ground. The inhabitants also enjoyed the music furnished by the 52nd band, which almost daily performed in the officers' square.

A large and imposing structure was now being erected upon the exact site where the former Government House stood. The present building, owing to its greater proportions, consequently covered more ground. The model was a handsome residence in the island of Jamaica; the plans were drawn up by a celebrated architect, who had formerly been acquainted with Sir Howard Douglas, under whose direct supervision the entire building was constructed.

As, for some time, New Brunswick was ruled by a military governor, Government House was so arranged that a military and civil staff could each occupy a separate wing of the building, while the main body was allotted to the family. It was well for the Province that Sir Howard Douglas was then at hand. The handsome and substantial edifice remains a lasting monument of grateful remembrance.

While public affairs are thus engrossing the attention of the country at large, the family of Sir Howard are now quietly enjoying their temporary home in the lower part of the town. Lady Douglas, beloved by all, is assisting and cheering His Excellency with all the energy of her nature. The young ladies are happy in their varied labors of love.

Lady Rosamond has not yet turned her thoughts homeward, save to quiet the rebellious thoughts that rise with occasional and twofold bitterness; she has the heavy trial before her; she drives away the mocking realities of the future. Vain are the hours wasted in useless repining. When Lady Rosamond made the disclosure to her companion, Mary Douglas, receiving the full and deep sympathy of true friendship, had she fully relieved her mind of its entire burden--its crushing weight? Ah, no! there was hidden deep in the most remote corner of Lady Rosamond's heart a secret which she would never reveal. Time would bring its changes. Her ladyship would return to her native home, and, amidst its gay scenes, pass a lifetime of seeming happiness; and the secret will burn its impress in characters of flame.

One evening Lady Douglas remained in her own apartments somewhat longer than her custom. Had prying eyes been active the cause might be assigned to the entrance of Lady Rosamond, who had joined her ladyship nearly an hour previous. On seeing the agitated face of the pale but beautiful girl her ladyship experienced a pang of deep remorse. She felt her strength deserting her, yet the task was to be accomplished.

"Rosamond, my darling," said the gentle lady, "I have received a letter from Lady Bereford, who, judging from the tone of the writing, seems to have some anxiety on your behalf."

This revelation afforded momentary relief to the high-born girl, who was, indeed, a lovely picture, reclining on a cushion at the feet of Lady Douglas. A shade of sadness rested upon her face, giving her the expression of a Madonna--a study for Raphael.

"Lady Bereford intimates, in touching terms, that I am to exercise a careful surveillance upon your girlish fancies," continued her ladyship, with slight sarcasm in her tone.

"Rosamond, my darling," cried she, by way of apostrophe, "I have every reason to place in you full confidence. I cannot see any ground for such intimation."

"Your ladyship is right," returned Lady Rosamond, throwing her arms around the neck of Lady Douglas, giving full vent to the feelings which almost overwhelmed her, adding, between tears and sobs: "I have always obeyed my father's wishes and will not shrink from my duty now. Gerald Bereford is worthy of a nobler wife than I dare ever hope to be. He has indeed conferred on me a distinguished honor, and I must try to make amends with all the gratitude of which I am capable."

Saying this the brave girl tried to force a smile, which, from its superficial nature, cost a great effort, adding:

"Your ladyship will have nothing to fear; my father's wishes are mine."

From the spirit of determination, which left an impress on the beautiful features of Lady Rosamond, Lady Douglas apprehended no need of interference. She knew that Lady Rosamond would fulfil her father's wishes. She was aware that the affectionate daughter would return his confidence, even at the greatest sacrifice a woman can make. The noble nature of Lady Douglas felt deep sympathy for her gentle relative--a vague uneasiness filled her mind. Some moments later when Lady Rosamond appeared in a rich and elegant dinner costume not a trace of emotion was visible. Its recent effects had entirely disappeared. Lady Douglas had found an opportunity to form an estimate of the strength of character which sustained the apparently gentle and passive maiden.

At the dinner table of Government House everyone seemed to vie in good humored gaiety and flow of spirited, animating conversation. Each tried to please. All clouds of despondency vanished upon this occasion. Sir Howard always set the example. Pressing cares of state, perplexing questions, and endless grievances, took speedy and ignominious flight when he entered the family circle. All was unrestrained pleasure and genial delight on this evening. Lady Rosamond was seated beside the gay and attractive secretary, who was endeavoring to engage his companion as an ally against the more formidable onset of Captain Douglas. She did fairly surprise the latter by the earnestness of her replies, her forcible expressions, and the weighty arguments upheld by superior judgment. Lieutenant Trevelyan, as he converses with Lady Douglas, betrays no outward feeling. He shows no preference for Lady Rosamond, being more frequently the companion and attendant of Mary Douglas, who, in trusting friendship, reposes in her young friend a happy confidence. Despite this assumed ease on the part of Guy Trevelyan, the keen interest hitherto exhibited by Mr. Howe has lost none of its freshness. The charm still lingers. All hope has not fled, though the light is in the uncertain future. In Lady Rosamond the well concerted plans of the secretary find no compromise. Dreading an exposure of her weakness she has thrown around her a formidable barrier which the most deadly shafts cannot penetrate. In the possession of this defence she can withstand the united efforts of a lengthy siege. Upon all those operations she can look grimly on and bid defiance. Mr. Howe felt this as he tried to force an entrance to the heart of this lovely maiden to wrest from her, if possible, a secret that would give a hopeful assurance to his projects. An incident shortly afterwards occurred which forever banished those thoughts from his mind, leaving no further room for doubt; still the fact cannot be overlooked, that the spirit which pervaded the private secretary of Sir Howard Douglas, was fraught with generosity and true manliness.

One evening as Captain Douglas and the latter were indulging in a quiet chat the conversation turned upon Lady Rosamond.

"She is indeed possessed of remarkable strength of character, which is the more surprising from the natural timidity and gentleness of her disposition," remarked

Captain Douglas.

"I have greatly admired her of late, and have, on more than one occasion tried to study the depths of her nature," returned Mr. Howe, with sudden earnestness. He was bent upon disclosing further plans to his friend when the latter exclaimed:

"By jove! Gerald Bereford is a lucky fellow, to win the Lady Rosamond as his future bride."

A look of startled surprise betrayed the excited feelings of Mr. Howe, leading Captain Douglas to remark:

"Look here, old chap, one would be apt to imagine that *you* were deeply smitten were they now to get a glimpse of your face."

Mr. Howe smiled.

"Yes," continued Charles Douglas, "her ladyship is to marry her cousin, Gerald Bereford, shortly after her arrival in England."

This was certainly a new aspect of affairs. Mr. Howe now viewed the matter in another light, yet he could not heartily respond. Vainly he strove to banish these thoughts, silently murmuring "poor Trevelyan!"

CHAPTER XII.
CHANGE.

We now arrive at the period when many changes are about to take place. The gayest and most gallant regiment ever stationed in Fredericton was under orders to be in readiness for departure. This was a source of much regret to the citizens, who shared in the extravagant scenes of gaiety so lavishly furnished. The sportsmen of Fredericton lamented the fact with deep regret. We cannot let this opportunity pass to relate an incident showing to what excess horse racing was carried in those days. Captain H----, an officer of the above named regiment, a true sporting character, owned a stud of the best thorough-breds in America. He annually spent an immense income in horse racing and various sports. In the meantime there lived in the city of St. John a coachman named Larry Stivers. If ever any individual sacrificed his entire heart and soul to the management, training and nature of horses, it was the self same Larry. Though possessed of limited means, no privation was too great in order to gratify such demands. A race was finally agreed upon between Captain H---- and this remarkable individual, which in the horse records of New Brunswick has no precedent, the case being unparalleled at home or abroad. One fine morning in March, 1826, the magnificent team of horses, driven by the captain, made its appearance in the market square, St. John. After the lapse of a few moments a second team arrived and was drawn up aside the former. No inquiry was made as to the ownership of the latter. Everybody recognized it as the turnout of Larry Stivers. But the most remarkable feature of the proceeding, that excited curiosity, was the slight construction of the sleighs. It could scarcely be conceived that they would stand the trying test of the proposed race. But they did. Each driver having purchased a bundle of whips, jumped into his seat. The word was given. Off they went at full speed, going the first nine miles over bare ground. The news spread over the city of St. John with almost incredible rapidity. Excitement filled the mind of everybody. No telegraphic despatches could furnish details as at the present. On they trotted side by side over the smooth surface of the St. John river, which course had been taken after the first nine miles. Whips were freely used upon the flagging animals. Sometimes Captain H---- kept ahead, in another minute Larry was quite a distance in advance. On, on the infuriated animals raced to the heavy lashes of their merciless drivers. Whip after whip was broken; still on they went over the glittering surface, the only sound the ceaseless crackling of whips and the ring of hoofs upon the still frosty atmosphere. About nine miles from Fredericton, as those heartless sportsmen were madly urging on their jaded beasts, a well-known lumber merchant of the town was accosted by the leader demanding a whip, which, one is sorry to acknowledge, was given. They had used the whole bundle, and mercilessly begged for more. Still on they came, the exhausted animals panting and ready to fall. The goal must be reached. Fredericton must be the only stopping place. One at least was to be disappointed. Four miles have yet to be passed. Larry Stivers is ahead, with visions of hopeful victory before him. He is suddenly stopped. One of the brave animals dropped dead on the spot. Hope instantly vanished. Captain H---- wins the race, while the former arrives shortly after his contestant with the dead animal upon the sleigh. Fredericton is reached. A distance of eighty-five miles is trotted in six hours and thirty minutes, inclusive of twenty minutes for rest and dinner. This wonderful feat caused general astonishment. Hundreds drove from Fredericton to meet the contestants, while crowds gathered to see the effect thus produced upon the poor exhausted animals. Soldiers were in attendance upon their arrival, almost dragging them up the bank. Being rubbed and dosed they were soon restored. The horse that dropped had been substituted for the famous "Tanner," and not having sufficient training was unequal to the task. The surviving animal, belonging to Larry Stivers, afterwards became one of the best and fastest horses in the Province. This incident is not introduced to interest horsemen, but merely to show how far men's judgment may be led astray by the force of such ruling passions.

To return to our narrative. Hearty demonstrations were participated in by the citizens in testimony of the appreciation of the military. Balls were given, dinners, speeches and testimonials. No efforts remained untried to express deep sympathy.

Great was the joy at Government House when Captain Douglas informed the family of Lieutenant Trevelyan's being transferred to the succeeding regiment. Colonel Trevelyan had obtained this change at the request of Sir Howard and Lady Douglas. Though a favorite in the 52nd regiment, Lieutenant Trevelyan's character did not harmonize with those of his brother officers--a circumstance that did not escape the notice of His Excellency. The matter formed the subject of correspondence between the latter and Colonel Trevelyan, resulting in the announcement previously made by Captain Douglas. Much delight shone on every countenance. Lady Douglas congratulated her young friend. Mary Douglas testified her joy with childish gaiety. Pioneer Johnnie looked forward to another sylvan pilgrimage with boyish glee. Merriment had exchanged places with murmuring and regret. The secretary alone remained in a state bordering on hesitation. He would indeed miss his boyish companion, yet the sense of his presence gave pain. Though not expressed by word or action, he was aware of the deep and passionate attachment which Lieutenant Trevelyan had formed for Lady Rosamond Seymour. He was aware of the hopeless result of this knowledge, and felt a sense of relief in the thought that changing scenes and new acquaintances might claim attention and heal the wound which otherwise would remain fresh and painful.

The arrival of the 81st regiment was, as customary on such occasions, celebrated by a general muster of the citizens.

The York County Militia presented a fine soldierly appearance. The grenadiers were indeed worthy of the tribute paid to their manly form and graceful bearing. Conspicuous was the rising favorite, Vivian Yorke. His flashing eye, regular features, broad, intellectual forehead, and firmly chiselled lips, received many compliments as he stood beside his companions. Lieutenant Trevelyan, in the military staff of His Excellency, also was not allowed to pass unnoticed. It was a remarkable coincidence that on this occasion, as the crowd bore down upon the company, Lieutenant Trevelyan was nearly in line with the young grenadier officer. A thoughtless young lady, standing near, exclaimed hastily to her companion: "Fanny, how much that young officer resembles Mr. Yorke." The remark being overheard by both parties, caused slight embarrassment, accompanied by a boyish blush from Lieutenant Trevelyan. Though an intimacy was formed between those young gentlemen, no allusion was made to the circumstance until many years afterwards, when Mr. Yorke was in England transacting some important political business, he was laughingly reminded of the affair by a gentleman in the prime of manhood--no longer a blushing young officer. Mr. Yorke and Sir Guy Trevelyan joined heartily in the joke, the former remarking that this young lady must have been colorblind in respect to their eyes. Many such comparisons were made rendering defective the perception of the fair judge, and causing much amusement to the assembled company. But this is a digression which the reader will excuse.

Lieutenant Trevelyan was now serving in H. M. 81st regiment under the command of Colonel Creagh--a veteran of Waterloo--who was highly pleased with the flattering testimonial he had received from Major McNair, relative to the irreproachable character borne by the young favorite.

A heavy cloud lowered over Government House. Its inmates were once more wrapped in gloomy thought. Mary Douglas already felt the pang of separation. Lady Rosamond was to return home. Her visit had been lengthened beyond the term allowed; now she must obey the summons without further delay. Painful thoughts crossed her ladyship's mind as she made the necessary preparations. Her fate was already sealed. She could not turn aside the resistless torrent that marked the course over which she must be borne by the skill of the fearless and merciless pilot, Lady Bereford.

In the outward conduct of Lady Rosamond none could detect the spirit which actuated her feelings. Lady Douglas closely watched every movement. Were it not for the emotion which the former betrayed on receiving the contents of Lady Bereford's letter, would it not have occurred to her to suspect the heart of Lady Rosamond. It was this circumstance which gave concern to Lady Douglas. She kept her own counsel, yet was impressed with the belief that Sir Thomas Seymour, in conjunction with Lady Bereford, was forcing her favorite into a marriage that was distasteful to her wishes. The longer her ladyship dwelt upon the matter the more deeply she felt concerned; but knowing the inflexible temper of Sir Thomas and the influence of Lady Bereford, she concluded that the case was indeed a hopeless one.

Mary Douglas was the only being to whom Lady Rosamond had confided the secret relative to her father's wishes. Some days preceding her departure the beautiful features of the young girl bore traces of grief. In the arms of her fond companion she had wept sad and bitter tears.

"This shall be the last exhibition of my feelings," vehemently cried Lady Rosamond, "you will never again see a tear of mine, at least from the same cause, but darling promise me now that you will never divulge my secret?"

"Accept my promise, Rosamond," returned Mary, impressing a fond kiss upon the lips of the gentle and loving girl.

The promise thus made was faithfully kept to be referred to in after years as a dream of the past which was still fresh in the beauty and loveliness of true friendship.

Lieutenant Trevelyan bore the knowledge of Lady Rosamond's departure with firm composure. He was kind, genial and entertaining. The strange and uneasy expression came and went with no remark save that it gave much annoyance to the kind hearted secretary.

The latter saw that no advances were made on the part of the young lieutenant. Her ladyship would depart while the story would remain untold.

It is needless to enter into the details attendant upon Lady Rosamond's removal from Government House. Sad and tender were the scenes. Mary Douglas could not repress the stifling sobs and outbursts of grief. True to the previous determination, her ladyship had schooled herself for the trying moment. Under the tender care of Sir Howard, the lovely girl took leave of Fredericton, leaving behind those whom she fondly loved. She carried with her many reminiscences of the scenes and trials through which she had passed never to be forgotten throughout her lifetime.

In the meantime a question arose in political affairs which required the mature deliberation of Sir Howard. The boundary dispute was now argued within every district with an earnestness that showed the importance of the cause. The present grievance had grown out of a former one.

In the treaty of 1873, the description of boundary limits between the United States and the Colonies was vague. Owing to a want of proper procedure, England and America merely took their limits from a certain point on the coast, one choosing to the right the other to the left.

The interior boundary was the watershed dividing the sources of the Connecticut and St. Croix rivers from those which emptied into the St. Lawrence. By this the Americans gained all the land bordering their own rivers, while the British had the banks of all the rivers extending to the sea coast. Breach after breach was made, yearly inroads upon British territory were effected, until the free navigation of the St. Lawrence was claimed, leaving the colonies without a frontier.

In the State of Maine, a hostile feeling influenced the entire population. A spirit of fiery independence asserted itself in the face of the British government. Sir Howard kept his eye on the stealthy movements of his disorderly neighbors. He was not to be outwitted by such aggressions; he was determined that neither Colonist nor American should transgress; his rights were to be respected. A New Brunswicker had been prosecuted for attempting to interfere. Equal justice was to be extended to all. The filibusters were not to be pacified; they abused England and her representatives in the most violent and abusive terms. The grievances of Maine must be redressed. Governor Lincoln ordered out the militia to the frontier, while an army of filibusters was ready to take possession of the territory. They thought to work a plan to throw blame upon Sir Howard, in the hope that the English troops might be led to engage in a conflict with the American militia; but the experience of the British representative served him aright, as on former occasions.

Baker, an unprincipled filibuster now resolved to force proceedings, rushed into British ground and tauntingly hoisted the American flag. At this juncture of affairs it was expected that English troops would interfere and a general fight would be the result.

Sir Howard had kept the troops at a respectable distance, where he could order them up at short notice; but he had no such intention. Imagine the surprise of both parties when a constable, having arrived, knocked down the flag and took Baker prisoner. Heavy imprecations fell upon such a course of conduct. Federal troops marched to the frontier, a circumstance of which the colonists took no notice. Sir Howard took further steps; he ordered the prisoner to be brought to trial before the Supreme Court at Fredericton, where he was found guilty, with sentence of a heavy fine.

Threatening attitudes were assumed by the leaders of this dispute, but to these Sir Howard paid not the least attention. Messages were sent by Governor Lincoln with urgent demands for Baker's release without any effect. They had to treat with one whose character was marked by firm determination. An American officer was also sent urging the necessity of the release of the prisoner. He was not granted an interview, but was kindly cared for in the mess-room of the 81st, where the officers gave him a hearty reception by a grand dinner, ordered expressly for the occasion. Despite the swaggering and menacing tone of this guest, the evening was spent in successive rounds of mirth and exciting gaiety. Songs, toasts and speeches greeted the ears of the envoy, and amidst these he almost forgot the object of his mission. At last the fine was paid. It was not until the matter was finally settled, by the decision of the king of the Netherlands, that comparative peace was restored.

This chapter now ends, having described the principal events that marked the year 1827.

CHAPTER XIII.
CHESLEY MANOR--MARRIAGE
OF LADY ROSAMOND.

We are again introduced to Lady Rosamond, now reinstated in the home of her childhood. A sense of gratitude is awakened within her as she fondly gazes upon the old familiar scenes surrounding Chesley Manor. The quaint old structure was an exact specimen of an English manor house in the early part of the seventeenth century, having been designed by an architect of the royal household in the reign of James the First, whence it still continued in the possession of its illustrious descendants.

The style adapted to the above named structure was more strictly domestic than defensive. It was built in quadrangular form, containing only one large court, upon which opened the stately hall, chapel, and principal apartments. Though not commanding the imposing aspect and grandeur of Bereford Castle, Chesley Manor had an air of true gentility in keeping with that of its owner. Lofty windows, reaching to the ground, looked out upon the gardens, which were enclosed by a high wall.

The period in which the present edifice was constructed was that of the best style of English architecture, contrasting the more elegant and graceful manor house with the frowning keep and embattled walls of the olden castle.

Surrey, with its old historic associations, was a fitting abode for the dreamy and poetic nature of the lovely, high-born maiden. The adjoining districts, with vale and meadow, had a pleasing effect. Long neglected parks and straggling decayed mansions, afforded ample scope for the fanciful flights of her ladyship's fond imagination.

Sir Thomas was indeed happy in thus having his daughter once more to brighten the home so long desolate and lonely. He enjoyed the perpetual sunshine of her bright presence. He loved to caress his beautiful child and admire her sweet and bewitching charms. Lady Rosamond seemed happy when in her father's presence. She returned his tender endearments with childish and playful gestures; she brought sunshine in her path in which the flowers of affection bloomed with luxuriant beauty. She was esteemed by the train of domestics and functionaries who performed the duties of the household. This fact somewhat conciliated the young mistress of Chesley Manor. Her grateful nature could not view these matters without feeling their import.

Wandering through the exquisitely arranged suites of spacious rooms which had been renovated with a desire to meet her approbation, Lady Rosamond could not but experience a pang of heartfelt sorrow. Parental love overcame her weakness. Sir Thomas alone possessed the key that gained access to her feelings. He alone could turn aside the channel of her resisting thoughts and mark the course for the tide of conflicting torrents as they surge madly on.

Maude Bereford is once more cheered in the daily companionship of Lady Rosamond. In their girlish and pretty ways those lovely girls form a pleasing picture to grace the interior and surroundings of Chesley Manor. Maude has a gentle and lovable disposition which wins the admiration of both sexes. Though not a beauty, she is truly beautiful--beautiful in heart, beautiful in soul. None see this mental beauty more clearly than the young mistress of the manor. The gentle nature and simple-minded heart of Maude Bereford sees in her cousin the sweetness and worth which are so fondly adored by her brother Gerald.

That Lady Rosamond sees in her future husband all that can make the heart truly happy is a source of constant delight to her loving cousin. Maude has not the keen perception of the nature of the human heart.

Lady Bereford was sanguine over the result of her diplomatic tact. There lay no obstruction in the path which she had marked out for Gerald Bereford. No rivals had given cause for offence. Lady Rosamond had readily encouraged the advances made by her suitor. It was now a settled conclusion. The fact had been communicated throughout the country. Sir Thomas had already received hearty congratulations on the brilliant prospects of his only daughter. The event was eagerly anticipated in the fashionable circles of high life. Many high-born maidens felt a tinge of jealousy as they listened to the brilliant preparations awaiting the marriage of the future Lord Bereford. His courtly manners, pleasing graces, and handsome appearance, were the comment of many. His proud privileges as peer of the realm, his princely castle and great wealth, furnished themes for eulogy.

While the great event was pending, and general curiosity was awakened in the course of proceedings, the Lady Rosamond alone remained passive. She calmly listened to the different reports of those to whom was entrusted the management of affairs with an ease that was perplexing in its simplicity. A genial smile repaid any effort to please. She gave advice with a gentle deference that surprised her most intimate friends and companions. With calmness and subdued feelings did her ladyship examine the costly satins and laces scattered in lavish profusion, and being in readiness to assume the most courtly and elegant costumes at the sanction of the fair enchantress. Maude Bereford was radiant with joy, the delightful prospect was at hand. Bereford Castle was to receive her dearest Rosamond. A splendid house was to be in readiness in the suburbs of London, where she would revel in the delights of fashionable society and the daily companionship of Lady Rosamond.

Gerald Bereford looked forward to the consummation of his hopes with fond solicitude. Having received from Lady Rosamond a quiet appreciation of his tenderness and deep love, he dared not to question closely the motives which actuated her. Sometimes he had momentary doubts concerning the entire reciprocation of her ladyship's trust and confidence, which caused considerable anxiety, but the sweet, pensive smile which asserted itself was sufficient to drive out a host of smothered grievances.

When Lady Rosamond promised to become the wife of Gerald Bereford she did so from a true sense of duty and affection towards her only parent. For him she would make the great sacrifice. Did the occasion demand, she would sacrifice her life on his behalf. In reality she had made such a test of her faith when she made her betrothal vow, bartering love, happiness, and life. Yes; life, with its true enjoyments, by this sacrifice, would become a mocking, bitter trial, to which even death were gladly welcome. Yet the noble girl shrank not from the task which the stern voice of duty had assigned. She would bear it without a murmur. None save Mary Douglas should know the depths of feeling of which her nature was capable. Gerald

Bereford would acknowledge the daily attention of a kind and dutiful wife. No human being should know a secret that was to her more than life--a soul within--a burning, smouldering fire, around which clings the shuddering form of outraged Hope. Lady Rosamond has kept her secret, therefore the writer will keep it in respect to her ladyship's inward sanctity. The reader may have gained it; if not, dear reader, you will in the end be rewarded for your patience by a disclosure. In the meantime let us follow her ladyship through all the perplexing moments of her unhappy existence, admiring the true courage and grateful sentiments which sustain her.

The day appointed for the eventful ceremony had arrived. Cards of invitation having been issued to the most distinguished nobility throughout the kingdom, a vast assemblage of expectant guests filled the seats and aisles of the ancient gothic cathedral in which the marriage was about to be solemnized. Happy smiles beamed upon all faces as they glanced around the handsome edifice so beautifully decorated for the occasion. Flowers and garlands were lavishly strewn around, scattered upon the floor, upon the steps, upon the way-side; literally all space was crowned with flowers. Gerald Bereford was truly a prepossessing bridegroom, worthy of loving and being loved in return. His truthful countenance was beaming with manly love. He was now ready to pronounce those vows which in his heart met a ready response. Lady Rosamond and her train of lovely bridesmaids have arrived. Hundreds of spectators are anxious to catch a passing glimpse of the beautiful bride as she is led to the altar by Sir Thomas Seymour, who gazes with loving tenderness upon the object so soon to be taken from his heart and home.

The feverish flush of excitement upon the transparent complexion of the bride lent additional aid to her matchless charms. Lady Rosamond is indeed a creature of surpassing loveliness. The soft texture of white satin that floats in bewitching folds of drapery around the faultless form is heightened in effect by an intermixture of costly lace and flashing jewels. The bridal veil, with its coronet of diamonds and orange blossoms, conceals the features so passive in the efforts to conceal the emotions which are struggling within the bosom of the fair one as she slowly utters those vows which, in accordance with her former resolve, she will earnestly strive to perform. Conscience awakens in her a deep shudder by setting forth painful convictions of promises given where her heart beats no response. But lady Rosamond felt relief from the thought of her efforts to do what she could to atone for this knowledge. Her husband would be happy in her presence if not her love. Those were the thoughts that occupied the lovely bride as she accepted the congratulations of the crowd who gathered around her. A pleasing smile greeted every one of the guests; even Lady Bereford was satisfied with the grateful acknowledgement. The bridegroom was a happy man. He adored his lovely bride. He looked upon her as the perfect embodiment of love and truth. Such were the sentiments that stimulated Gerald Bereford as his wife was received into society with all the eclat attendant upon rank, wealth and beauty. Her appearance on several occasions was hailed with universal delight. Her unassuming manner, childlike disposition and elegant grace made friends at every footstep. Jealousy found no favor in the wake of Lady Rosamond. Her presence was sufficient warning to the green-eyed monster to make hasty retreat.

Lord Bereford took a fond interest in his newly found daughter. He had always loved Lady Rosamond as his own child. She reminded him of the lovely sister who shared in his youthful joys. Maria Bereford was the favorite sister of his early days; her daughter was a tender link in the chain of memory. Lady Rosamond fully returned the affection borne her by Lord Bereford. She found a strange relief when sitting by his side listening to the stories which brought before her vivid conceptions of her childhood and its happy past never to return--the days when her heart was free to roam in its wayward and fanciful nights full of ardour and the bouyant aspirations of unfettered youth.

Gerald Bereford proved indeed a tender and loving husband. His heart was always ready to upbraid him if he were not ready to meet the slightest wish of his young wife. Every kindness that could be bestowed on Lady Rosamond daily suggested itself to the mind of her thoughtful husband. He was only happy in her presence--she was the sunshine of his heart, of his life, of his soul. Without Lady Rosamond this world was a blank--a region "where light never enters, hope never comes." Nor was the fact unknown to the dutiful and amiable wife. It grieved her deeply to witness such an exhibition of true love and tenderness without its receiving equal return. With heroic bravery she endeavored to reward her husband by little acts of thoughtful kindness greeting his return from the turmoil of political struggles. Pleasing surprises often met his eye when least expected. Many pretty trinkets made expressly for his use, by the fair hands of Lady Rosamond, were placed in careless profusion around his private apartments. These trifling incidents were an hundredfold more worth to Gerald Bereford than the most well-timed and flattering acknowledgments of the many who daily courted his friendship. Thus did her ladyship strive to make amends to her husband without having recourse to deceit. She returned his caresses, not with a fervent love, but with a feeling that such generous love exacted her sympathy. In the tenderness of her heart some recompense must be made. Would she ever learn to love her husband as he indeed deserved to be loved? When would the hour arrive when she could say: "Gerald, I love you with my entire heart and soul; I live for you alone; none other can possess the great love I bear for you, my husband." Those questions were frequently present in the mind of the devoted wife of Gerald Bereford. But he knew it not. He was in blissful ignorance of the fire within as he fondly dreamed of the pleasing graces of his lovely wife. He had no reason to be otherwise than happy.

Lady Rosamond Bereford was above suspicion. She had no desire to possess popularity outside her own household. The flattery of the opposite sex was lost upon her. The false smile of base and unprincipled men found no favor in the sight of her ladyship. She discountenanced many practices sanctioned by the usages of good society. Virtue was the true criterion upon which was based her ladyship's judgment.

It is almost needless to add that congratulations reached Lady Rosamond from the family at Government House in Fredericton. It was not a matter of surprise to Lady Douglas. She had too much confidence in the character of her relative to doubt her resolution. Mary Douglas fondly clung to the hope that her companion would, by some unforeseen power, avert the threatening blow. She betrayed no astonishment. Though daily expecting the sickening news of the marriage, the private secretary of Sir Howard almost staggered under the sudden weight of anxiety which possessed him when Captain Douglas made the startling disclosure, with the accompanying remark: "Jove! I always said that Gerald Bereford was a lucky fellow."

The thoughtful gaze of Mr. Howe as he stood in mute and silent astonishment, raised a laugh from his companion, with the addition of a second remark, implying that her ladyship must have made sad havoc upon the heart of a certain individual, judging from the effect produced by the announcement of her marriage.

True indeed! Lady Rosamond had made havoc upon the heart and affection of a ***certain individual***, as Captain Douglas roughly remarked, but not the one to whom he made direct allusion.

The heart that suffered most will be the last to acknowledge. "Heaven pity poor Trevelyan," murmured Mr. Howe.

CHAPTER XIV.
NEW FRIENDS--THE 81ST--SOCIAL RECREATION.

Fredericton society was now becoming amply compensated for the loss sustained by the departure of the 52nd Regiment. The gallant Col. Creagh had become a general favorite. Waterloo, with its bloody scenes and brilliant victory, was still fresh in his memory. He never wearied in relating these with fond pride, while his heart was fired with an enthusiasm that stirred every vein with renewed patriotic impulses. The gentlemanly conduct that marked the officers of the 81st, soon won the esteem of the citizens, and placed them on confidential and friendly terms within a short time after their arrival. Though not distinguished by the sporting propensities of their predecessors, the general tone of society received a loftier impetus, social intercourse on a moderate basis was the general feature of the present. Balls and parties were of greater importance than the sports of the turf or field. It must not be inferred the 81st Regiment was quiet and inactive from the facts thus stated. On the contrary, they were gay, dashing and animated, full of the vigour and energy of military life; but the comparison affects them not when we say that the sporting reputation of the 52nd Regiment was unprecedented in military records. Among those deserving notice was Jasper Creagh. He was a winning and agreeable youth, displaying much of the daring and military spirit of his distinguished sire. Many hearts beat faster when they listened to the manly voice of the young soldier. Within a very short space of time an intimacy sprang up between the latter and Lieutenant Trevelyan, who more than sustained the very flattering reputation forwarded by Major McNair.

Jasper Creagh found much pleasure in the company of his newly made friend, while the observant Colonel was well pleased by the preference which showed such judgment on the part of his eldest son.

Frequent allusions were made to the marriage of Lady Rosamond. This brilliant match had afforded much subject for gossip in the higher social circles. Lieutenant Trevelyan quietly listened to the earnest congratulations showered upon this union with apparent interest, often replying to the inquiries of Jasper Creagh with marked concern. His secret was unknown, he could brave the matter with heroic fortitude, while perhaps in after years, time will have effaced those fond memories. It was a bitter trial, but had he known that hearts more liable to succumb to the frailties of nature had borne up bravely against the struggling conflicts of feeling, the thought would have afforded some relief.

Captain Douglas in his boisterous jocose remarks had unconsciously been the means of aiming many unerring and merciless shafts at the heart of the despondent lieutenant. Mr. Howe, on many occasions, would generously have forced his companion to desist, but the sacrifice would have been too great. It were better that the secret remain untold even at the expense of a few such stabs.

In spite of the maneuvering conversational tactics of Mr. Howe, Captain Douglas could not resist the vein of humor which flowed in incessant remark upon those with whom it came in contact. "Lady Rosamond made sad havoc in Fredericton," was his endless theme. "Look at Howe, judging from the length of his face the matter has assumed a serious aspect. There is some doubt as to the exact state of Trevelyan's heart. If the face be taken as an index to the mind, we will pronounce his case as a milder type of the same disease."

Many like jokes were passed around by the incorrigible Charles Douglas, but to all Guy Trevelyan was invulnerable. He betrayed no sign of the inward tempest raging within, save by the almost imperceptible expression which had attracted the scrutinizing eye of the generous hearted Mr. Howe.

The band of the 81st was a great source of amusement to the citizens. It daily furnished music on the Officers' Square, which was entirely free to every peaceably disposed citizen. Another attractive feature was the frequent sights of numerous barges rowing up and down the river. The gay strains of music that floated upon the air, the flutter of bright-colored pennons, the waving of streamers, bright faces, merry hearts, and joyous song, made the scene both enjoyable and imposing. Frequently the excursionists landed on the islands above the city, enjoying the hours in roaming around the woody precincts, in merry conversation, outdoor sport, or the pleasure of the dance. Thus did the citizens spend the greater number of the pleasant summer evenings in the indebtedness of their military friends.

The band-master stood high in the esteem of all ranks and classes. Mr. Hoben had indeed succeeded in filling the position occupied by his predecessor in relation with the Philharmonic Society, sparing no pains in the instruction of every member.

The above named musical organization had now attained a degree of proficiency that was manifest on every public appearance.

Mr. Yorke, of whom mention was made on several former occasions, was a great favorite in musical circles. His taste was consulted on the arrangement of many programmes intended for public dinners, and such demonstrations as called forth a ready response from the general public. The musical abilities of Vivian Yorke were afterwards kept in constant requisition.

The various schemes pushed forward by Sir Howard Douglas for the advancement of the welfare of the Province were heartily endorsed by the people. Steady advances were being made in every pursuit, while that of agriculture was foremost. Societies were formed with a view to adopt measures the most favorable for the advancement of a cause to which all others were secondary in the estimation of Sir Howard. York County Agricultural Society, at that time, was composed of a body of influential members, whose places have never since been filled by any who took such a deep interest in those matters. Such names as those of the Hon. Messrs. Baillie, Odell, Street, Black, Saunders, Bliss, Peters, Shore, Minchin, and many others, grace the pages of the yearly reports issued by the society.

An event occurred about this time which had considerable effect upon the social atmosphere of Fredericton. The old part of the officers' barracks, known as the mess-room, was completely destroyed by fire. It was in the depth of winter, on a very cold night, and many experienced much exposure and fatigue. The promptness displayed, both by military and citizens, may still be remembered by some of the older inhabitants. On this occasion a poor soldier would have been suffocated were it not for the presence of mind displayed by Mr. Yorke, who, on hearing the groans of the distressed man, burst in the door and bore him out amid stifling volumes of smoke and flame.

Much inconvenience arose from the fact of being deprived of comfortable quarters at such an inclement season; but the citizens soon had the pleasure of seeing the officers' mess-room of the 81st stationed in the brick building situated on the corner of Queen and Regent streets, where they had procured temporary accommodation until another and more commodious building should be erected on the site of the former. It was only by such fires that the town of Fredericton succeeded in presenting a more imposing appearance. Small two-story wooden houses, with smaller door and windows, occupied Queen street with an air of ease, seeming to defy progress, and only to be removed by the devouring elements which occasionally made havoc upon those wooden structures.

The present season was remarkable for the many skating tournaments which were held upon the ice in the vicinity of Fredericton. Among those who distinguished themselves were Captain Hansard, an officer retired from the service, and a young gentleman afterwards known in connection with the Crown Land Department and later as a member of the Executive Government, yet an active member of the Legislative Council. The most astonishing feats were performed during the time thus occupied. The officers of the 81st were superior skaters, among whom was Major Booth whose remarkable evolutions gained great notoriety. It is a matter of question whether the feats of the present day to which our attention is sometimes directed, could in anywise compete with those of the days of which we write. Lieutenant Trevelyan had acquired a proficiency in the art that was worthy of admiration. In this healthy pastime he took secret delight. It afforded moments when he could steal miles away and give himself up to those quiet reveries from which the dreamer finds relief. To a sensitive and poetic mind, what is more enjoyable than the silent hours of solitude when the soul is revelling in the delights of idealism; its sweet commune with kindred spirits; its longing and fanciful aspirations? Who that is not possessed of those precious gifts of the soul can realize the happiness that Guy Trevelyan derived from this source? He could, as it were, divest himself of earthy material and live in the ethereal essence of divine communion. In those flights of bliss the loved form of Lady Rosamond was ever near. Her presence hallowed the path whereon he trod. None others invaded the sanctity of this realm of dreams. One soul was there--one being--alas! to wake in one realty.

Mary Douglas was at all times a true sympathizer. She always took a deep interest in her friend Guy. She liked to sit beside him and recall little scenes wherein

Lady Rosamond took part. Her merry ringing laugh showed the purity of the mind within. Together they spent many hours in interesting and amusing conversation. Not a thought save that of true friendship entered the mind of either. From this alone arose the full confidence alike reposed in each. Mary Douglas was even more beautiful than Lady Rosamond. Her features were formed as regularly as a model of an Angelo; her expression might be a life-long study for a DaVinci, a Rubens, or a Reynolds. Yet such beauty had not power to fan anew the smouldering fire which consumed the vitality of Lieutenant Trevelyan's existence. On the other hand this lovely girl saw not in her companion anything that could create any feeling akin to love. Such was the entire confidence thus reposed that they were amused at any trifling remarks of those who daily summed up what evidence supported their conjectures. Frequently Mr. Howe turned his attention to the affairs of the unfortunate lieutenant, vainly wishing that such an attachment might be formed and likewise reciprocated. He was certain of the fact that Guy Trevelyan was worthy the hand of the most distinguished and beautiful. He was aware that Sir Howard entertained the highest regard to the son of his old friend Colonel Trevelyan who, as a baronet and gentleman, had a reputation worthy his manly son. The arguments advanced by Mr. Howe were by no means lessened when he wondered if Lady Rosamond could possibly have gained the secret which possessed Guy Trevelyan. He held too high an opinion of her ladyship to harbor the thought that she would triumph in the conquest thus gained on the eve of her marriage with Gerald Bereford. Ah no! Lady Rosamond could not have known it. So reasoned the thoughtful secretary.

In the meantime Lady Rosamond is enjoying the constant whirl and gaiety of London life. Her husband is immersed in the broil of parliamentary affairs. As a representative of his native borough, he is responsible for every grievance, real or imaginary, under which his constituents are daily groaning. The party with whom he was associated was daily becoming unpopular--a crisis was at hand--a dissolution was expected. Another appeal to the country would probably take place. Her ladyship was not a politician; she understood not the measure so proudly discussed by the wives of statesmen and representatives. Still she could not but feel a desire to share in the interests of her husband. In the bustle and turmoil of busy life she felt grateful. Excitement fed her inquietude; it bore her along upon the breast of the dizzy waves. It was well that Lady Rosamond was thus occupied. She gave grand

and sumptuous dinner parties, and entertained her guests with balls on a scale of princely magnificence. Her luncheons were indeed sufficient to cheer the most despondent and misanthropic. Gaiety in its varied forms predominated over Lady Rosamond's establishment.

Gerald Bereford was proud of the homage poured at the feet of his beautiful wife. Her praise was music in his ears. He listened to the flattering courtesies with childlike pleasure. Her happiness was his. Often when overcome with the cares and anxiety of public affairs a smile from her ladyship had a charm like magic. A quiet caress was sure to arouse him from the deepest apathy.

Lady Rosamond strove hard to repay her doting husband. Every attention was paid to his wishes. He knew not what it was to suffer the slightest neglect. Gerald Bereford was happy. His happiness was often the subject of comment of the associates of his club. His wife's unassuming beauty, her grace and virtues, attracted many who were solicitous to cultivate her acquaintance.

"How did you manage to secure such a prize, Bereford? She is the most beautiful woman in the United Kingdom," exclaimed a gentleman to Gerald Bereford, after being introduced to Lady Rosamond at a ball given by the French ambassador, where, without any conscious effort, she had been pronounced the most attractive amidst a bewildering array of princely rank, wealth, dignity, youth and beauty.

None could deny the assertion. The rich and elegant black velvet robes worn by her ladyship displayed the beautiful transparency and form of her snowy arms and shoulders. Flashing jewels lent a glow to the lovely face, reflecting their purity and priceless worth.

In the midst of her greatest triumphs Lady Rosamond felt her misery the most unendurable. Then she experienced the cruel mockeries of the world; *then* she felt pangs that the glare and display of wealth must cover--that the tribute of homage vainly sought to satisfy. At those moments a picture of never-fading reality would flit before her mental vision in mocking array--a picture in which her ladyship knelt with expressive and silent gaze at the feet of the stern monitress, Duty, whose defiant scowl denies appeal from the speaking depths of the mournful dark eyes. Two forms are discerned in the background; the foremost reveals the features of Gerald Bereford casting fond glances towards the kneeling figure in the foreground. Duty wears a smile as she beckons his approach with tokens of deep appreciation. There still lingers another form. Whose can it be? Can we not recognize that face, though indistinct, in the dim outline? Duty steps between and intercepts our view. This is the picture from which Lady Rosamond vainly tried to withdraw her thoughts, repeating the consoling words with saddened emphasis: "Everything is ordered for the best."

CHAPTER XV.
POLITICAL LIFE.

While Lady Rosamond received the homage of a thousand hearts and plunged into the ceaseless round of busy life, her husband was engaged as a fierce combatant in earnest conflicts in the political arena within the limits of Parliament. Enclosed by vast and wondrous piles of stately architecture, the champions fight for their respective boroughs with untiring energy and vehement fiery ardour. The ministry, headed by the Duke of Wellington, stood much in need of all the force which it could bring to bear upon the rallying strength of the opposing element. Among the latter was arrayed Mr. Bereford. His penetrating judgment and shrewd activity were considered an important acquisition to the ranks of his colleagues. His masterly and eloquent harangues never failed to force deep conviction and prove the justice of his principles. Even Lady Rosamond felt a secret pride in listening to those earnest appeals which disclosed the honest motives by which they were actuated. Though not gifted with the brilliant powers displayed in the conversational genius of those women who had evidently devoted much attention to the study of politics, her ladyship tried to feel an interest in the measures for which her husband had devoted many of his waking hours, his superior intellectual powers, his fond ambition. In this source she seemed to find a sense of relief. She never flinched when any exaction was required. If she could make some recompense for such pure and fervent love, no matter at what cost or sacrifice, gladly would the conscientious principles of Lady Rosamond accept the terms. Her marked concern and unremitting attention failed not to elicit admiration from the Premier, who, despite his stern, disciplined nature, had not forgotten to pay tribute to the attractions of a beautiful woman. The Iron Duke indeed showed a decided preference for her ladyship. He was charmed with the sweet, unassuming, and childlike manner of the young matron, and took delight in contrasting these with the glaring and ostentatious demeanor of these high-minded and profound women with whom he daily mingled.

Lady Rosamond repaid the gallant Duke for such attention. She loved to engage him in earnest and animated conversation, and watch the fire that kindled the soul within by the light emitted from the deep flashing eye. She felt a deep interest in the stern old warrior from the endearing associations which his memory had woven around her. While in Fredericton her ladyship had heard many stories in which her friends had also figured in close relation to the hero of a hundred fights. Sir Howard Douglas had oftentimes entertained his family circle with a recital of such scenes. The friend of Sir Howard, Colonel Trevelyan, was also an actor in the great drama. But the last personage could not possibly cause any tender interest to the mind of Lady Rosamond.

Gerald Bereford was opposed in principle to the present administration. He formed one of the strongest leaders of the opposition. His heart was in the work before him; he would not flinch from the responsibility. His haggard countenance often gave evidence of the spirit which influenced his actions; yet he wearied not. A mild reproof from his lovely wife would for the while have some effect, when he would devote all his leisure to her comfort and pastime, being fully repaid by the most simple caress or quiet smile.

Early in the next year an event followed which had a great effect both on political and social life. His Majesty, George the Fourth, had passed away from earth. Among those within our acquaintance few there were who deeply regretted the circumstance.

Lady Rosamond, in writing a friend, said: "We cannot indeed entertain any lasting regrets for one who inflicted such misery upon one of our sex. The unfortunate queen and her tragical end inspires me with a feeling bordering upon hate towards the author. As women we must feel it, but as women we must forgive."

Thus was the matter viewed by her ladyship, who now looked forward with happy anticipation to the approaching and brilliant pageantry. The "Sailor King" sat peacefully on the throne of England. In the days of her childhood Lady Rosamond loved to climb upon the knee of a handsome nobleman--in truth a gallant prince. Lovingly did she nestle against his manly breast with eager, childish confidence, throwing her beautiful silken ringlets over his shoulders in gleeful pride. Many times had she kissed the lips of her royal patron, while he playfully designated her his "White Rose of England." Among the many beautiful trinkets she had received at his hands none were more valuable or precious than the jewelled locket bearing the simple inscription "William," appended to a miniature chain, which she had always worn around her neck in grateful remembrance. The kind-hearted prince had won the lovely child. Kind memories can never be obliterated from kind hearts.

Lady Rosamond in after years never forgot the sailor prince of her childhood days. The old admiral was proud of the attachment thus formed in his early career. He had entertained towards the generous prince a warm regard. In naval cruises they were often thrown in company, while on more than one occasion Sir Thomas had granted leave to obtain the service of his young friend for a lengthened cruise.

It is not, therefore, a matter of surprise that Lady Rosamond hailed with rapturous delight the accession of the sailor prince as William the Fourth of England. Her hopes beat high as she thought of the approaching ceremony when she would once more be recognized by her old friend. Has she outgrown his memory? or has he kept her still in view through each successive stage of life? Many were the speculations formed within the mind of her ladyship as she made the elaborate preparation necessary for the intended reception. The day at length arrived. The king and queen were to receive the nobility of the realm. Dukes, earls, viscounts, marquises, baronets, with all the titled members of their families, were to pass in array before the conscious glance and smile of majesty.

The royal reception chamber blazed with dazzling splendour. Titled courtiers in costly dresses of crimson, purple, and violet velvet, embroidered in gold, glittering with the many orders upon their breasts, while the jewelled hilt of the golden scabbards flashed in dazzling rays of light. These lined the apartment or moved to and fro at the summon of royalty. Ladies of honor were grouped at respective distances from their sovereign mistress ready to obey her slightest behest. Their costly robes, courtly grace, and distinguished appearance, befitted the noble blood which ran through their veins as proof of their present proud position. To a stranger the scene was impressive. On first entering the train of attendants and military display is sufficient to quell the most stout hearted. Passing along with as much dignity as the person can, he is announced in loud stentorian tones by the lord chamberlain, who glances at the card thus presented. Then advancing towards the throne, kneeling down, kissing the back of His Majesty's hand, and passing along in the train of his predecessor forms the remaining part of the ceremony. During this time hundreds will have taken part in these proceedings, happy in the thought of having received a respectful bow from the grateful monarch in return for the deep and almost overpowering embarrassment that possesses the one taking part in those imposing ceremonies.

The rising blush on Lady Rosamond's cheek showed the excitement that stirred the depths of her inward feelings. She was carried back to the happy child days when no shade hovered near; when no bitter concealment lurked in the recesses of her joyous heart; when her fond plans were openly discussed before the sailor prince with intense merriment and glee. Vainly she sighed as she thought of what might have been. Though in the present the inference was distasteful, her ladyship could not dismiss the subject. As she stands quietly awaiting her turn in the order of presentation, let us once more picture the beautiful face and form which have won our entire sympathy.

Lady Rosamond has lost none of the beauty hitherto depicted in her charms. She is still lovely as when described while a guest at Government House. Her cheek has lost none of its roundness; the outline is full, striking, fresh and interesting; the expressive dark eyes have lost not their usual brilliancy, save a mournful tenderness that is more often betrayed than formerly; the lustrous black hair is wantonly revelling in all the luxuriance of its former beauty. Time nor experience has not the ruthless power to desecrate such sacred charms. Lady Rosamond has yet to rejoice in these; she has yet to pluck the blossoms of happiness springing up from the soil of buried hope where seeds had been scattered by the unseen hand of Mercy. Well might Gerald Bereford have been fond of his wife as she approached the "Sailor King," in her train of white satin and velvet sparkling with diamonds, with a grace bespeaking ease, trust and dignified repose. The announcement of Lady Rosamond Bereford afforded striking proof of the warm-heartedness of his majesty, showing he did not forget his former white rose of England. His eagle eye detected the small jewelled gift almost concealed within the breast of her ladyship, as she lowly bent down to kiss the hand of her sovereign. A beautiful blush overspread the features of Lady Rosamond as she felt the directed gaze. "Your ladyship has not forgotten the sharer of her childhood joys," exclaimed His Majesty with expressive smile.

A deep blush succeeded when the kneeling suppliant recovered sufficient self-possession to reply. "Your Majesty will pardon this occasion to acknowledge the great honor conferred by this tender allusion to a loving and loyal subject."

In her blushing loveliness, Lady Rosamond received a fragrant and beautiful white rose from the hand of her liege sovereign as expressive of the desired continuation of his former regard and endearment. This was truly a remarkable moment in the life of her ladyship. She felt the true force and depth of friendship. If the favor of her monarch could give happiness, would she not exercise a large monopoly? Yet there was happiness enjoined in the ceremony. His Majesty was happy to meet his former friend and companion. Her Majesty the Queen was happy to find one in whom her husband found so much to admire. Gerald Bereford was truly happy in having such royal favour extended towards the lovely being upon whom he lavished his fond love.

These circumstances gave some relief to lady Rosamond and taught her many lessons through suffering to which she could return with thankful gratitude for the bitter trials so heavily imposed. Sometimes a feeling of remorse took possession of her ladyship as she looked upon the face of her husband and fancied that there rested a yearning, wistful look, a lingering for her truer sympathy. She sometimes felt that her husband also cherished his vain regrets, his moments of bitter conflicts when he tried to smother the unbidden thoughts that would thus arise. These fancies often roused Lady Rosamond to a sense of her duty with wholesome effect.

This mark of royal favor was not lost upon Lady Rosamond. Her Majesty expressed a wish to receive the king's favorite among the ladies of her household. But the tearful eyes of the beautiful matron forbade any further mention. The German propensities of Queen Adelaide would not force any measure thus proposed. Lady Rosamond had full access to the royal household, receiving the confidence of her royal patroness with true grace.

Now began the struggle for Reform in the Parliament. Throughout the kingdom arose the cry of Reform which had been echoed from the second French revolution. Among all classes arose the war note of Reform. It sounded loud and high. It was borne over the continent. Nothing but Reform. Reform of the House of Commons was the subject discussed at every fireside.

Affairs had now reached a political crisis. The Duke of Wellington, with his unrestrained and high-bred principles of conservatism, could not brook such an innovation upon the time-honored laws and customs of the British constitution. He could not favor a faction that would countenance the spoliation of England's hitherto undimmed greatness and national pride. Hence arose a new ministry under the united leadership of Earl Grey and Lord John Russell. In Gerald Bereford the supporters of the Reform measure found a zealous adherent. He seemed to lay aside every other consideration in advancing the scheme which lay so near his heart. Lengthy and private consultations were held between the latter and his sincere friend and adviser, Earl Grey. Days and nights were passed in fierce and endless controversy in the House of Commons.

This was the only point in which Lady Rosamond failed to convince her husband of the injury sustained by such constant turmoil and anxiety involved in these measures. When she quietly endeavored to reason upon such a course of conduct he smilingly replied: "My darling, duty calls me and you would not see me inactive when the demand is so imperative? Surely my beautiful rose would not like to have the breath of slander attached to her husband as guilty of cowardice or desertion from the ranks of his party? Ah, no, my darling," cried the earnest politician, preventing his wife's retort with the tender kisses of a true and ardent love. It did indeed seem strange that the more earnestly Lady Rosamond pleaded with her husband the more firmly did he resist, and, if possible, the more ardent he became in his attention. Lady Rosamond felt a strange and unaccountable desire to interfere with the plans laid down by Gerald Bereford. Many times she urged upon Earl Grey the necessity of moderation, and, with a vehemence foreign to her nature, strove to impress him with prophetic visions of anxiety, doubt, and fear. Her ladyship was somewhat reconciled by the resignation of the Premier, who, in his joking manner, attributed his want of success to the hostile attitude of the wife of his friend, Gerald Bereford.

But the conflict was kept up with renewed energy. The Reform party were not to be thus easily outwitted. They were still sanguine. During the period when the ministry vacillated between the Conservatives and Whigs, the spirits of the latter never drooped. Victory was the watchword that attached itself to the Reform party. Victory was the cry of Gerald Bereford as he labored day and night with untiring zeal, utterly regardless of the ravages thus made upon his hitherto robust constitution. In this exciting struggle the young politician was unconscious of the deadly and venomous growth taking root within under the baneful effect of negligence and over-taxed powers.

CHAPTER XVI.
NEW BRUNSWICK.

The capital of New Brunswick was the scene of more than usual excitement. Extensive preparations throughout the higher classes of society indicated that some very important event or events were about to take place. Extravagant purchases made in the several stores where were displayed dry goods, intimated that the fair sex looked forward to the approaching festivity with intense and joyous anticipation.

New-year's eve has arrived. Happiness expresses itself in rippling smiles beaming upon all faces. Every citizen has cause for rejoicing. The commodious structure planned under the supervision of His Excellency, Sir Howard Douglas, is now ready for the reception of a numerous assemblage of guests. The family are reinstated in Government House, happy in being once more able to extend their far-famed hospitality as on former occasions.

Nothing was wanting to make the present reception one of the most gorgeous in the social records of provincial life. Every window in the entire building was brilliantly illuminated in the most beautiful colors of every hue and in a charming variety of scenes. There were represented the western heavens at sunset in crimson and gold; the rising glories of the approaching monarch shown on the eastern hill tops; scenes of classical beauty shone in bewitching effect. Any attempt to particularize fails in the very effort. Suffice to say Government House blazed, not in the spontaneous spirit which displayed itself when the former building succumbed, but by the heightening aid of artistic skill and design. From a distance the sight was truly beautiful. Many gazed with unwearied eyes anxious to behold a view which might never again be afforded them. The incessant peals of merry sleigh bells seemed to harmonize with the merriment and gaiety of the guests as they hurried to their destination. The array of rank, wealth, youth and beauty thus assembled are never again to be realized. Every colony in His Majesty's domains in America was represented. Every one holding high rank or title was present. Lady Douglas with kindling eye glanced through the different rooms and pronounced the affair a decided success.

Mary Douglas experienced a feeling of sadness while drawing a comparison between the present occasion and one in which Lady Rosamond was an honored guest. She could not but feel a deep yearning towards her old friend--a fond and tender longing to embrace the beautiful Lady Rosamond Bereford.

The drawing-rooms reflected credit upon those who assisted in the decorations. Brilliant colors, banners, emblems, mottoes, flags, pennons, and coats of arms were intermingled with an eye to harmony and graceful effect.

The military precedence on every hand shewed the spirit which influenced Sir Howard and his distinguished family. Nearly all the gentlemen of the household were distinguished by their uniform. Every attendant was in uniform. Soldiers lined the grounds; soldiers kept hourly patrol; soldiers executed every command. The social atmosphere of Government House breathed of a true soldier-like element. The ladies felt its influence as they took delight in listening to the chequered scenes amidst the lives of the many veterans who sat at their table.

The 81st now graced the evening by a numerous body of officers with the gallant Colonel Creagh foremost in the assembly. The genial countenance of the old veteran, his sparkling eye and animated gestures found ready entrance into many hearts. Conspicuous were Jasper Creagh, now attached to the regiment as holding a lieutenant's commission, and his friend Trevelyan, now promoted to the rank of Captain, and still enjoying the unbounded good will and confidence of superiors and inferiors.

The faithful secretary still sustained his former resources for enjoyment and festivity. He had made himself agreeable to many fair ladies, acting the part of a gallant attendant, but his heart remained unimpressed, often a source of keen enjoyment to Captain Douglas, who vainly tried to captivate his friend in many ways. Mr. Howe was a distinguished and fine-looking gentleman, remarkably tall and straight, while the keen glance of his dark eye was sufficient to convince one of the powers of penetration forming such weighty proportion in the make-up of his character. His olive skin formed a pleasing contrast to the pearl white complexion of the beautiful daughter of the household, as they mingled together in the dance. The sparkle of that lovely eye was enough to drive the adoring suitors to distraction, yet Mary Douglas coolly withstood their ardent gaze. Dance and song mingle in successive round. Youth and age alike join in the fairy scene. Arch glances pass from courtly cavaliers to beautiful maidens who "blush at the praise of their own loveliness." The rustle of silken draperies sound to the ear as unseen music at the hand of the warbling genii. Robes of spotless purity and gossamer texture flit around, keeping time to the merry ringing silvery peals of girlish merriment. Such are the scenes that greet the eye and ear in roaming amid the gay throng at Government House, Fredericton, on the New Year's Eve of 1828.

It would be a difficult task to make particular mention of the aristocratic matrons; still it would be a great injustice to pass over a matter of so much importance. In fact, by some, the married ladies bore off the palm for beauty and intelligence. Of a certainty the comparison excepted the ladies of Government House, there being none who could compete with Mary Douglas, her beauty being of a superior type.

At the ball a married lady of rank wore diamonds valued at a cost seeming fabulous. Others followed in the wake of such extravagance by wearing necklaces, bracelets, head-dresses, ear-rings, and brooches, in almost unlimited profusion. Add to this the magnificent array of Sir Howard's supper table, its glittering plate in massive style, its enormous chandeliers, its countless train of liveried attendants, and you can then only form a very faint conception of the first ball given in the present Government House, nearly half a century in the past!

Truly this was the chivalric age in the history of the capital of New Brunswick--the age when proud knighthood was the ruling passion in the breasts of the sterner sex, when true heroic bravery was the quality which won the maiden fair, when the breath of slander could not be tolerated without calling forth a brave champion on behalf of the wronged. This is the age that has passed away never to return. Progress and Reform are the two great powers combined to crush out all traces of those bygone days. In united action they ruthlessly wipe out every vestige or lingering relics of past greatness. Nothing must stand in opposition to their will. Reform suggests, Progress acts--Reform suggests the removal of all old landmarks--Progress assists in the accomplishment. By such means, and through successive stages, did those days pass away, now to be reviewed, as a beautiful dream of the past.

Leaving this point we will proceed with the facts of the story.

The day following marked an event of much greater importance than that of the preceding evening--it was important to all--all classes were afterwards to be benefited by the great boon thus conferred on the people of New Brunswick. Every parish and county had reason afterwards to rejoice in the great work of this auspicious moment.

On New year's day of this year was opened the College at Fredericton. The Charter had been procured by Sir Howard after having withstood a storm of violent opposition, under which an ordinary spirit would have sunk in hopeless despondency; but the iron will and calm judgment of the wise statesman and ruler had outlived the fury of the opposing element, who now reaped the reward of his indefatigable labors by the accomplishment of the great work.

The king showed his sanction by conferring upon this Institution the name of "King's College, New Brunswick," while to Sir Howard he assigned the honor of being its first chancellor, in acknowledgment of the great service thus rendered to the cause.

In this office His Excellency was duly installed on the present occasion. Divine service was performed as the first ceremony. The professors and students were in their places. Members of the legislature and the royal council occupied seats, while the public thronged the building to the utmost capacity.

Great and heartfelt was the burst of applause that greeted Sir Howard as he took his place: greater still, when he announced the intention of the king in conferring his name upon the College. The expressive features, high, broad intellectual forehead, earnest eye, benign countenance and honest smile perhaps were never more significant of the earnestness that pervaded every thought and action of the gentleman, scholar, and soldier, as when he uttered sentiments which shall be cherished through after ages, so long as King's College shall remain a monument to the memory of the best and greatest man that ever trod the soil of New Brunswick.

Let us make use of his own words: "I shall leave with the College," he said, "I trust, for ever a token of my regard and best wishes. It shall be prepared in a form and devoted to an object which I hope may prove a useful incitement to virtue and learning; and at periodical commemorations of the commencement it may serve to remind you of the share which I have had in the institutions and proceedings of a day which I shall never forget."

Nor did this friend of education ever forget his promise. The Douglas Gold Medal is still competed for though many years have rolled between the time when the first and last were presented. The distinguished donor has passed away, but his pledge remains. Memory fondly clings around the deeds of Sir Howard and throws over them a halo of light that will shine with increasing splendor as time lengthens the distance between.

The boundary question still assumed a troubled and unsettled state. Many complaints were laid before his Excellency, but he calmly resolved to grant no concessions. He treated every messenger with polite firmness. Congratulations poured in from the Governor General from Canada and the British Minister at Washington, regarding the cleverness and ability displayed on the occasion. At last it became evident that no direct conciliation could be effected between the disputants. Another course must be adopted. An arrangement was agreed upon between the English and Americans that the matter be left to arbitration, to the decision of the king of the Netherlands. In such knowledge the people felt and saw a common dread, a common anxiety, a gloomy foreboding. Such knowledge brought the painful idea of separation. Sir Howard was appointed to prepare the case for presentation. His presence was imperative in England. A heavy blow fell like a death knell on the future hopes of the colonists. Their true friend, sympathizer and ruler was about to take leave. Many mourned his departure as that of a father or brother. Their friend in prosperity and dire adversity; he who had struggled with the calamities and worked for the advancement of his people, their interests and direct benefits, was now to embark for his native land.

Regret was depicted on every face as the colonists moved in large bodies to return grateful recognition for the zealous labors spent in their behalf. Every society took active measures in showing their mingled regret. Tears rained thick and fast as many old friends grasped the hand of Sir Howard, murmuring a last God bless you. The kind-hearted soldier could not but feel deeply when he witnessed such hearty demonstrations, yet he had hopes of returning to New Brunswick. He cheered the people with such remarks and strove to make the least of the matter.

Nor was the family of Sir Howard less to be regretted. Their kind hospitality,

generous hearts, and unassuming dispositions, had made many friends in Fredericton and throughout the Province.

Lady Douglas strove to conceal her regret with many well-timed remarks. Mary
Douglas lovingly lingered among the well-remembered walks and paths where she
had spent peaceful and happy days. The lovely spring-time which she had looked
forward to, with its songs of birds, bright sunshine, lovely flowers, and green fields,
had come again, but not for her enjoyment. Other ears would listen to the warbling songster--other forms would sit in her accustomed seats and enjoy the pleasing sunshine--other hands would pluck the lonely flowers blooming in beauty all
around--other footsteps would roam over the soft green grass that gently raised its
head as she tripped lightly along in former years. *These* were the friends of Mary
Douglas, truly the child of nature. Birds, flowers, fields, sunshine, rain, and storm,
were the constant companions of the gifted and beautiful student. The warble of
the birds was to her of more worth than the most bewitching strains of an English
opera; flowers taught lessons more inspiring and sublime than the most profound
theological discussion. Verdant fields and bright sunshine were constant reminders
of Heaven's choicest blessings and never-failing truth, while the stormy conflicts of
nature's elements taught the heart a wholesome lesson in the thought that life has
its changing moods, its bitter conflicts, its merciless storms.

Sad was the heart of the dreamer as she wandered for the last time amid these
never-to-be-forgotten haunts. Tears dimmed her lovely eyes and trickled down her
cheeks. The scene was too sacred for other eyes. She had started off alone, wishing to pay the last tribute of respect to her silent friends in a manner becoming the
solemnity of the occasion.

We leave Mary Douglas in her sylvan retreat and follow other members of the
family in their tender leave-taking.

Miss Douglas echoes the same spirit as her sister, but with less poetic eloquence
and fervent inspiration. She looks upon the faces of many dear young friends and
feels a deep pang of sorrow as their tears mingle with her own. John Douglas, no
longer a mischievous, romping, and noisy boy, but an engaging and attractive young
gentleman, ready to enter the army, takes a hearty leave of his former schoolmates
and companions with sincere regret, bearing with him their united wishes for his
future welfare and success in life.

It would be an endless task to enumerate the bitter repinings and tender leave-taking between each member of the family, and the numerous hosts of sincere friends who pressed around them, eager to wish God speed on the journey. Suffice to say, amid the last parting word, the last pressure of the hand, and the last fond embrace, the beloved family of Sir Howard Douglas took their last glimpse of Fredericton, dimmed by their fast falling tears, as the steamer slowly passed from the wharf, whence issued the plaintive strains of "Auld Lang Syne," to be borne ever after in the memory of those who listened to the last parting tribute wafted from the shores of Fredericton.

CHAPTER XVII.
REGRETS.

Though most of those in whom we have taken such deep interest have left the Province far behind, we cannot bear the thought of following them until more fond ties be broken that binds them to our native home. Ah! were we to consider every fond tie, there could be no hope for separation. There are ties which bind the heart as lovingly as those of friendship, there are ties which cling while we breath the inspiration of every page within the universal volumes of Heaven's choicest productions--the great book of nature--the teacher and refiner of the soul. This is the tie which clings to us through the medium of holy thought, inspiring, elevating and cheering.

Among those who most deeply felt the departure of the inmates of Government House, none were more reserved in their demonstrations than Captain Trevelyan, who calmly watched each successive step in the order of preparation with a quiet reserve that to the uninitiated would appear as void of feeling.

But the brave and handsome officer showed not the fathomless depths and feelings of his true heart, which throbbed with a renewed emotion. With a sense of utter loneliness he lamented the bitter misfortune which had been his attendant since he had left the peaceful home of his fatherland. Mary Douglas, his kind friend and companion, had been as a gentle and loving sister to raise for a time his flagging spirits. Mr. Howe had ever been at his side to show unceasing acts of kindness and brighten those dark hours with a tender but inexpressive sympathy. Captain Trevelyan could never forget the motives which actuated these, still he did not exhibit any outward show of gratitude save by a firm and passive confidence.

Knowing the true nature of such friendship, Mr. Howe would have experienced deeper regret at parting were he not aware that he would meet Captain Trevelyan early in the following year.

Left to the undisturbed quiet of his own thoughts, Captain Trevelyan formed many plans regarding his future career. A work was steadily going on within while he attended the duties devolving upon him in connection with his military life.

It had always been the true aim of this soldier to discharge his labors faithfully and with a desire to please. His genial nature and generous heart gained the popularity of the entire regiment. Not only did he treat his superior officers with profound respect but his inferiors as well. Every subordinate officer and private loved to meet his friendly smile. Every one vied in doing some act that would receive his approbation. Truly did Colonel Creagh make the following remark to a distinguished General, who was inspecting the troops: "If ever man were born who possessed not a single enemy, I believe that man is Captain Trevelyan."

"I believe you," returned the General, "goodness is stamped upon his handsome face, but seldom is it so clearly defined as to insure such general approval."

"Sometimes," added the Colonel, "I have doubts regarding the serious intentions of our friend. It has been whispered that he begins to weary of the service. I have not had sufficient reason to confirm the truth of the statement, but I shall feel much dissatisfied if it prove correct. Sir Howard Douglas always maintained that Trevelyan is a scion of the old stock, that he possesses the same qualities that distinguished his father. It would indeed be a source of regret were all to be disappointed by his retirement," said the Colonel, in a tone of deep earnestness.

"If the family resources are large he may have sufficient reason for such an act," ventured the General interrogatively.

"Sir Guy Trevelyan," said the Colonel, by way of explanation, "owns a fine old estate in Hampshire, which yields a moderate income. His only son will be his direct heir, and Captain Trevelyan can at any opportunity enjoy the ease and retirement of private life."

"I should not be surprised were he to avail himself of the departure of the regiment," exclaimed the general, adding, "there is not much distinction now to be gained in the service. Captain Trevelyan might remain an honorable officer in His Majesty's service for years to come and not attain the position marked out by his distinguished parent."

Many remarks were thus applied to this officer by the gallant colonel of the

81st Regiment. Every sentence showed not only the high esteem in which Captain Trevelyan was held by the veteran of Waterloo, but the fears entertained by the latter in regard to his rumoured retirement.

Not long after the above conversation took place Fredericton was to witness another departure--the gallant 81st, under orders, were to be relieved by the 1st Battalion of the Rifle Brigade. The same formalities of interchanging regrets were to be passed between those departing and the citizens. The same congratulations were to be presented in appreciation of the high esteem entertained towards the entire regiment in the presentation of testimonials and other marks of respect.

The morning preceding the departure of the company to which Captain Trevelyan was attached, afterwards formed an important one in his life. Colonel Creagh's fears were realized by intimation from Captain Trevelyan with intention to make application for a discharge immediately on his arrival in England.

After long and grave deliberation he had fully made up his mind, while a letter received from his sister gave twofold assurance of the great delight which such news communicated to the family.

As this young girl will now be introduced to the reader, we take the liberty of inserting the letter, showing the tenderness of feeling existing between the brother and sister, the fond anticipation breathed through every sentence, and the deep interest manifested in the friends of the absent one.

Frequently did Guy Trevelyan re-open the envelope and bring forth the precious missive, written in a delicate feminine hand, containing the following:--

Trevelyan Hall, near Winchester, Sept. 19th, 1830.

Dear Brother Guy,--

Your fond letter of the 20th was received in due time, conveying the most delightful news that ever was written. How can I await your dear presence? Really it seems almost too much happiness to realize that you will once more return home to remain. Papa writes that he warmly approves of your decision, intimating that I must have been instrumental in procuring such good fortune for us all. I dare not dream too fondly lest by some means I may be disappointed; but, dearest Guy, once restored to us, our delight will be unbounded.

You must not expect to have a very long letter this time, as I cannot settle my thoughts to think of aught but yourself and "The Restoration." If the second be not of such universal display as the one so grandly portrayed in history, it is doubtful whether the sincerity attending the latter be not of a more lasting nature and one showing the true affections of loyal and devoted hearts.

I had almost forgotten to mention that I have frequently met Mary Douglas, who is, at present, visiting her friend Maude Bereford, at the Castle. Also, had the pleasure of being introduced to your friend Mr. Howe, and feel a deep interest in him on your behalf. Imagine my delight when he informed me of his intention to accept your invitation to remain with us for a few days on your arrival. It seems that I cannot remember anything. I must not forget this time to say that great anxiety is expressed and felt at the Castle regarding the failing health of Lady Rosamond's husband--Mr. Gerald Bereford. For some time past he has sadly impaired his constitution by taxing his powers beyond endurance, and when almost too late, he withdrew from political life. Great sympathy is extended Lady Rosamond who seems very despondent. Medical advice suggests change of climate, and I have heard that they intend to spend the winter in Italy. Not wishing to give any more news until I see you at home, dear Guy, and having nothing further to add but our love,

I remain your expectant

Fanny.

Fanny Trevelyan's letter had a double effect upon the mind of the recipient. It involved both happiness and despondent gloom, and unconsciously had struck a tender chord which vibrated with redoubled sadness in its deep sympathy.

Why do the waking echoes of the past take cruel delight in presenting to the mind visions which otherwise would be laid aside in a retired recess or a secret chamber sacred to the relics of other days and other scenes? Why are those realities to present themselves in merciless and mocking array to gloat upon our sufferings with fiendish delight? These are questions only to be answered when the causes which call them forth have ceased to exist.

Captain Trevelyan's retirement was the subject of much concern for the officers and men. Many discussions arose as to the motive. Lieutenant Creagh remonstrated, but to no purpose. As the slow sailing ship bore the gallant regiment across the Atlantic, hope reigned supreme in many hearts. Friends and home greeted them on arrival. At Gosport, Captain Trevelyan took formal leave, having received the strongest proofs of sincere friendship existing between man and his fellowbeings.

Great was the joy that awaited Guy Trevelyan as he once more entered the fine old park enclosing the grounds of "Trevelyan Hall." His mother, a staid and stately English matron, forgot all dignity as she threw herself fondly into his arms. Fanny, the pet of the household, clung to her brother with tightening embrace, showering him with kisses pure as her maiden heart. Nor was the dutiful son less tender in his expressions of joy, as lovingly he gazed upon the fair girl seated with her arm upon his shoulder. He could scarcely realize that the little girl of twelve was now the lovely maiden of eighteen almost matured into a gentle and loveable woman. In her sweet childish manner Guy Trevelyan found much to admire. The firm, steady gaze of her deep blue eyes had a power to rivet the attention of the beholder, that puzzled him. He knew from the calm and earnest tenor of his sister's manner that her heart was unfettered by any deeper attachment than those of family ties. In the bitterness of his feelings he thanked Heaven for this fond assurance, fervently praying that the love of his pet sister would never be given where it would never be returned.

He now listened with eager curiosity to the affairs of Lady Rosamond. Her husband had indeed, when too late, listened to her urgent admonitions. He had resigned his seat in parliament when his physical powers were a mere wreck of his former self. Disease had crept in by stealth and was only too truly realized by the deep ravages thus made--by the wasted and emaciated form--the feverish cheek and sunken eye.

The noble sympathetic nature of the dutiful wife felt a severe shock as she daily was brought face to face with the dreaded fact--the awakening reality of her husband's condition. Every care that could be bestowed by the hand of woman was lavished upon Gerald Bereford with unceasing and untiring devotion. No duty was too troublesome, no wish was slighted, except that which urged her ladyship to be more attentive to her personal wants. Every sacrifice must be made that can possibly give returning health and strength to the future lord of Bereford Castle. No bitter repinings now possessed the heroic woman. Her whole being was thrown into the scale to balance the opposing weight which crushed her husband's almost lifeless existence. The voice of one who repeatedly made the halls of parliament ring with deafening applause was now with an effort heard by those standing near.

It was when such trouble bore heavily that Mary Douglas opened her heart towards her friend Lady Rosamond. She came unbidden to offer such service as was in her power to perform. She silently watched by the side of Gerald Bereford with that gentle caution so needful when suffering is apparent, or when an interval of pain or depression is to be guarded against as a thief in disguise.

Not a single expression ever passed between those friends with reference to any thing that happened in Fredericton. Mary Douglas was careful to avoid any allusion to circumstances which might call up a sudden host of by-gone fancies which, ere this, should be consigned to the remotest regions in the realm of utter oblivion. She was now the friend and sympathizer of Lady Rosamond Bereford, not the childish maiden as when first introduced, but a lovely, gifted, talented and accomplished woman, whose mind matured with her years. Time has not lain heavily on her hands, she having labored assiduously in exercising those talents committed to her keeping. In after years we find the following: "Her gifts were so varied that she was both a composer and musician, a novelist and poet." The friend of Lady Rosamond Bereford was not to be affected by the emotions of Lady Rosamond Seymour. The past was a sealed casket, forever sacred to the intrusion of the present. This was the state of feeling that existed between those noble women as they ministered to the wants of Gerald Bereford.

What fervent prayers were offered for the dutiful and self-sacrificing wife as she tried to win a smile from the patient invalid. What grateful love went forth to her as she pressed the lips of her uncomplaining husband. In sickness as in health she had never seen his frown. His life had been a constant source of happiness. Lady Rosamond had been the day-star which illuminated his path with undimmed lustre and brilliancy. In her presence he felt not the weight of suffering that at intervals seized his exhausted frame. As symptoms of the disease began to abate and recovery was expected, her ladyship, accompanied her husband to Italy, where they had intended to remove some time previous, but were prevented by a relapse of the invalid.

CHAPTER XVIII.
SIR HOWARD DOUGLAS.

In order to follow up the brilliant career of this great man while connected with the administration of New Brunswick, we will endeavor to give a few facts to prove the marvellous ability he displayed in carrying out his plans.

On the passage homeward Sir Howard and family encountered many dangers. During the whole voyage there was kept up a constant gale, sometimes threatening the destruction of the rudely constructed brig of war named the *Mutine*. Amidst these daily mishaps and perilous exposures the Douglas family maintained the utmost self-possession. Sir Howard was always ready to offer advice and assistance with a coolness that nerved the whole crew, and gave fresh hopes at the darkest moments. During the six weeks that elapsed, while braving the dangers of the deep, Mary Douglas never lost an opportunity to make the most of the occasion. She became interested in the stormy elements, learning lessons that served her to breast the struggling conflicts of life. Observation was largely developed in the mind of the gifted maiden. Nothing was presented to her eye that did not afford food for study and reflection.

The joy with which they were received in England was boundless. Friends gathered around with heartfelt demonstrations. Sir Howard was once more surrounded by many of his former companions. The Duke of Wellington gave him a hearty welcome, while statesmen could scarcely refrain emotion on beholding one who had taken such deep interest in the welfare of the nation and showed such firmness and decision in the boundary question. But another more distinguished honor awaited him. The University of Oxford were ready to recognize such greatness by conferring the degree of D. C. L. Sir Howard was called upon to be present at the commemoration of 1829, where crowds jostled each other to get a glimpse of this honored man. Patriotism has been, throughout history, the leading spirit governing the Universities of Great Britain and the present occasion proved no exception. Students were animated by the presence of a true patriot. Cheer upon cheer greeted the announcement of Sir Howard. Applause was boundless as he received presentation from the public orator. That the spirit which prompted such action on the part of this dignified body may be seen, we insert the following oration, taken from the life of Sir Howard Douglas:

Most illustrious Vice-Chancellor, and you, learned Doctors,

I present to you a distinguished man, adorned with many virtues and honors, belonging to military and civil affairs, as well as to literature--Howard, a Knight and Baronet, a worthy heir of the latter order from a renowned father, the former richly deserved from his own king and that of Spain; a member of the Royal Society of London, on account of the fame of his writings; for many years the Governor of New Brunswick, followed by the admiration and favor of his country and the reverence and love of the Province; lastly, Chancellor of a College in that Province, built under his care and direction, to which its patron, the king, gave his name and a University's privileges. Behold the man! I now present him to you that he may be admitted to the degree of a Doctor of Civil Laws for the sake of honor.

Further comment upon the above is unnecessary, it being sufficient to convince one of the degree of popularity which Sir Howard had attained.

The next place in which he plays a most conspicuous part is in the presence of royalty at the Dutch court, where he was received with all the honors his rank, position and claim demanded. His Majesty entered in a lengthy and earnest conversation regarding the important question now to be settled by his decision. Sir Howard stated clearly every circumstance in connection with the affair from beginning to end. To every question he gave a prompt reply, showing the clearness of judgment by which every argument had been maintained. In order to explain why such a question should be brought up forty-seven years after the treaty had been signed,

he showed that it was founded on some indefinite or ambiguous clauses of the treaty of 1783, but not proposed until 1820. Here was a delicate point for His Majesty
to settle without giving offence to either English or Americans. But Sir Howard was
resolved to support the claim which contended for the rights of his nation--for justice and for truth. He was not desiring territory, but protection and security to the
interests of his people, ***security*** to prevent the Americans from claiming the privileges of the St. John river or classifying the Bay of Fundy rivers with those emptying
into the Atlantic. However, a decision at length was given which did not meet the
wishes of either party, but the matter was set partially at rest.

Soon afterwards Sir Howard was engaged in discussing the cause and events of
the Belgian insurrection. He showed to the British Government the design which
France had contrived to her aggrandizement by the dissolution of the Netherlands,
and urged intervention on the part of the British Government. The measures taken
in determining the strength of the Dutch territory and the trouble thus averted
which must have involved war and bloodshed, secured the hearty thanks of the
English monarch who acknowledged the debt of gratitude in terms of deep sincerity. The colonists were now awaiting Sir Howard's return with great anxiety,
watching his movements with deep concern. Hope once more filled their hearts
as news spread abroad that their ruler was making preparations to return to New
Brunswick. But a new source of uneasiness arose. The Home Government raised a
question abolishing the protection on colonial timber. Sir Howard was aroused to a
sense of the situation. By the abolition of such protection the trade of New Brunswick and the other colonies would be ruined, while the Baltic trade would reap the
benefit. Was he to tamely submit to measures injuring the resources of the people
whom he represented? No, he would appeal in a manner that would have public
sympathy. Hence was produced the well written pamphlet bearing his name, setting forth the grievance in a way that could not fail to prove the justice of the cause.
Every point was discussed with clearness and based upon the most reliable facts and
statistics. Newspapers took up the subject and complimented the author in the most
flattering terms.

A general excitement was now raised and the question was discussed on every
side. In the House of Commons it gained much popularity. Great was the joy of Sir
Howard when the result of his work was announced by the defeat of the govern-

ment. This proved the patriotism of Sir Howard. He could not sacrifice the interest of his country to those of himself and family. He purchased his country's welfare with the resignation of the governorship of New Brunswick!

Where do we find such true nobility of character, such brilliant genius, and such unsullied virtue? Well might the Colonists have exclaimed with one voice when tidings conveyed the news of Sir Howard's resignation:

"He was a man, take him for all in all,
We shall not look upon his like again."

However, some recognition must be made to show their gratitude to one who had made such a sacrifice. Meetings were held in different parts of the Province resulting in a general subscription towards the purchase of a valuable service of plate which was presented him in England, accompanied by an address, breathing the spirit of heartfelt regret at the loss of their much beloved ruler. Sir Howard never forgot this circumstance. He often referred to his stay in New Brunswick with feelings bordering on emotion. Years afterwards his heart beat with quickening impulse as he fondly recognized the familiar face of a colonist or received some cheering account of the welfare of the people. Through the remaining years of his life he never ceased to keep up a faithful correspondence with several of his former friends, particularly the Rev. Edwin Jacob, D. D., who received the presidency of King's College through his kind patron,--the tie of friendship which bound them was only severed by death.

Much more might be said regarding this great man, but we must now leave him to the active duties of a busy and useful life, surrounded by his family in the comforts of an English home and enjoying the true friendship of the philosopher, the historian, and the poet. Among the most intimate in this list was Sir Walter Scott--the friend of Mrs. Bailie, the foster mother of Sir Howard. Doubtless the name of Douglas was sufficient to awaken in the mind of the Scottish bard a feeling worthy of the friendship of Sir Howard. Together they spent many hours in conversing upon the scenes which had formed subjects for the poet's pen and awakened a deep veneration for the legends of Scottish lore. Perhaps in no other way can we better pay a parting tribute to the memory of Sir Howard Douglas than by inserting the following letter which had been forwarded when the latter had arrived from New Brunswick:

"Abbotsford, Near Melrose, 21st July, 1829.

"***My Dear Sir Howard***,--

"I have just received your most welcome letter and write to express my earnest wish and hope that, as I have for the present no Edinburgh establishment, you will, for the sake of auld lang syne, give me the pleasure of seeing you here for as much time as you can spare me. There are some things worth looking at, and we have surely old friends and old stories enough to talk over. We are just thirty-two miles from Edinburgh. Two or three public coaches pass us within a mile, and I will take care to have a carriage meet you at Melrose Brigley End, if you prefer that way of travelling. Who can tell whether we may ever, in such different paths of life, have so good an opportunity of meeting? I see no danger of being absent from this place, but you drop me a line if you can be with us, and take it for granted you hardly come amiss. I have our poor little [illegible] here. He is in very indifferent health, but no immediate danger is apprehended. You mention your daughter. I would be most happy if she should be able to accompany you.

"Always, my dear Sir Howard,
Most truly yours,
Walter Scott."

Here is an instance of genuine simplicity and hearty friendship existing between men of like nature. The true greatness of Sir Howard was appreciated by one whose themes of poetic beauty and fervent patriotism kindle a glow of inspiration that will burn undimmed while time shall last. And now we close this chapter by bidding the noble, great and good Sir Howard Douglas a fond farewell!

CHAPTER XIX.
TREVELYAN HALL--THE ARRIVAL.

The fine old building, well known to the surrounding country as Trevelyan Hall, was indeed a true specimen of an English home. Its present owner had, notwithstanding the fact of his being abroad in service, spent much means to make it a home-like and delightful residence. Its situation added to the other resources in gaining for "The Hall" a wide-spread reputation.

The extensive park contained some of the best wooded ground in the county of Hampshire. Its fine streams afforded means of enjoyment for those who devote their pastime in angling and other such health-giving recreation. Its gardens were carefully cultivated, showing much neatness and elegance, though not affording a varied extent of scenery.

Captain Trevelyan's return was now to be associated with new and varied interest in the interior and exterior management of this pleasant home. Fanny Trevelyan was cheered by the hope of her brother's presence. Company would now be entertained in a manner creditable to the former hospitality which distinguished the Trevelyans. The handsome and elegant apartments assigned to the daily use of the inmates in nowise deteriorated from the exterior prospect. The extensive drawing-rooms, in which were arranged, with tasteful effect, rich furniture, gorgeous carpets, and all those beautiful collections of art, requisite to adorn the home of the great and refined. The inviting library with its massive display of well-lined shelves, the cheerful breakfast room with its eastern aspect, the countless retreats, balconies, verandas, and summer houses, formed a pleasing feature in the every-day life, pursuits, and recreations of this affectionate family. Home was the spirit-like influence which was infused in every feeling, thought, and action. A sense of ease and comfort was enjoyed throughout the entire household. Despite the difference of rank, wealth, and dignity, the poor dependents felt a warm and devoted confidence in their high-born superiors. In the sweet and childlike Fanny Trevelyan there was a subtle magnetizing influence which compelled acknowledgment. In her kind and loving heart was much room for the troubles and daily cares of the dependents surrounding the estate of Trevelyan Hall. Many acts of kindness were performed in a quiet and childlike way that was indeed pretty to see.

The only daughter of Colonel Trevelyan was a maiden of a rare and striking character. Her gentle disposition was sufficient to win admiration irrespective of the purity and noble qualities of her mind. Though eighteen summers had lightly flown over the head of this lovely girl, her manner was that of a sweet, intelligent, lovable, and sensitive child. Sweetness of disposition was truly the coloring most profusely portrayed in the character of Fanny Trevelyan. In this fact lay her great delight upon Captain Trevelyan's return. Upon this fact was based the happy expectation of seeing the generous-hearted Mr. Howe. From this source she found all that contributed to make life pleasant and enjoyable.

The possessor of those charms had no great claim to personal beauty, yet she might be called beautiful. The regular features of her small and well formed face were devoid of any distinguishing lineaments, the deep blue eyes had a quiet, earnest light, which often shone with increasing brightness, when accompanied with the expressive smile so often bestowed upon those who dwelt within and around "The Hall."

As sometimes one hears remarks paid to beauty called forth by blushes, surely in this instance we can fairly claim the compliment due Fanny Trevelyan, whose maiden blushes indeed made her appear in truth very beautiful--of the beauty which shall last when all other shall fade--of the beauty which flows from the heart, kept fresh in the daily performance of those duties that spring from the impulses of a beautiful soul. Thus might be classified the type of beauty which adorned the sister of Captain Trevelyan--beauty of disposition--beauty of mind--beauty of soul.

During the last two years a friendship had sprung up between Fanny Trevelyan and Maude Bereford. They had studied for a short time under the same masters, from which fact arose the present attachment. A striking similarity of disposition was noticeable between those friends, yet, in many respects they were widely different. Though Fanny Trevelyan was so deeply sensitive, childish and engaging, there was a depth of character underlying these which found no comparison in Maude Bereford, the former possessing powers of thought and reflection, which were entire strangers to the mind of the latter. In the preferment of Lady Rosamond, they were of the same mind. While on a visit to the Castle, Fanny Trevelyan had received many proofs of affection from its beautiful young mistress. She took much pleasure in the company of Maude Bereford in strolling amid the lovely gardens, but experienced keener delight in listening to Lady Rosamond's description of scenes in New Brunswick rendered so dear by being associated with her brother who was still indeed her great regard. Many times Fanny Trevelyan tried to form various conjectures concerning this beautiful woman, wondering why she had such an influence that was more powerful when removed from her presence. She wondered if her brother Guy felt the same powerful influence as herself. He had never expressed any decided opinion in favor of her ladyship, yet she did not consider the fact as of much importance; but he had not shown in any manner, nor by repeated inquiries, any betrayal that would lead one to suppose that he entertained any regard whatever for the lovely being.

Fanny Trevelyan was now busied in matters of great importance. Preparations were being made for the reception of Maude Bereford, Mary Douglas and Mr. Howe. Then she would hear still further of New Brunswick life--its pleasures and its inconveniences. Gaily did she perform the many little offices left to deft fingers and untiring patience. Maude had availed herself of the temporary absence of her invalid brother and his devoted wife. Three weeks were to be spent in the society of Trevelyan Hall. Fanny Trevelyan had a little secret project in her mind which gave much pleasure. She would be in a position to introduce Maude Bereford to the notice of her brother Guy. With girlish glee she anticipated much from the circumstance, wondering in what way her friend might be received at the hand of the last named gentleman.

On the other hand Captain Trevelyan had *his* plans to mature. Without consulting his sister's opinion, he had a secret pleasure in the hope that his ever true friend might find much to admire in the young girl who was soon to be their guest. He had not the slightest wish to enter on any schemes by which his loved sister might be complicated. Fanny Trevelyan was fancy free. It was his fond hope that she remain so many years to come. Bitter experience taught Captain Trevelyan a lesson from which he could draw many useful hints and resolves. He was careful to guard against any exposure to which his loved sister might be subjected.

Amid these doubly laid plans the inmates of the hall welcomed their visitors, in whom were also included Captain Douglas. The sincerity of the latter was expressive in the humorous and hearty congratulations showered upon the genial host.

"Trevelyan, old boy, you are a mighty fine specimen of the old school! Egad, what would the Frederictonians say could they look in upon you now," exclaimed the incorrigible Charles, with the ruling passion uppermost, while he threw himself upon an easy chair in a free and jovial manner.

"I am inclined to think that they would not be favorably impressed with such a wholesale exhibition were each one to repeat the same performance as yourself," retorted Mr. Howe, assuming an air of nonchalance.

"Ah, I see how it is with my honored friend," once more ventured Captain Douglas, "he already is maturing plans to place me at disadvantage before I have fairly secured entrance to Trevelyan Hall; but," added the speaker, with an air of playful menace, "old chap the tables may turn, as they did many a time in Fredericton."

Much as Mr. Howe regarded his friend, Charles Douglas, he wished that the last remark had not been made. Though it were said with the ease of unconscious and humorous gaiety, the quick glance of the secretary saw the instant effect. This was the only point on which he remained reticent to his bosom friend. They had been together for years. They had grown from childhood together, yet Captain Trevelyan's secret must remain a secret. Were it known to Charles Douglas, he would have cherished it with a sanctity becoming him as one whose whole lifetime marked out the strait laid down by the great poet: "where one but goes abreast." But the hospitable host was in his gayest mood. Everything contributed to make the reception a flattering one. Fanny Trevelyan was at ease among the old friends of her deeply beloved brother. Mary Douglas was in ecstacies of delight upon thus meeting Guy Trevelyan. On several occasions she was deeply sad when referring to the troubles of Lady Rosamond, but seemed to feel hopeful in the return of Gerald Bereford's health and strength. Maude Bereford was playful, entertaining and happy. A more pleasant party were never gathered at "The Hall." Lady Trevelyan was a dignified and reserved woman, possessing much judgment and coolness of decision, but added to these were qualities which endeared her both to her family and all those who made her acquaintance. It was with extreme pleasure that she contributed a share in the entertainment of those friends who had extended such kindness to her only son when placed among strangers in a distant land. By every possible means within her power, Lady Trevelyan lavished both gratitude and affection upon the beautiful daughter of the distinguished family who had shared their hearts and home with the handsome young lieutenant when first deprived of the society of his own happy household. Such was the disposition of Lady Trevelyan that these tokens of disinterested friendship could never be forgotten, but steadily shone as a bright light to cheer her daily path, undimmed by any darkening visions of disappointed hopes or vain delusions.

This happy family have realized their parents' wishes. Captain Trevelyan's retirement was urged by an earnest entreaty on the part of his mother. By it he could attend to the numerous requirements of the estate, which had lately become an onerous duty devolving upon Mrs. Trevelyan. The faithful steward of the family had grown old in the service and not capable of managing the business as in the days of his prime. Yet the fact only added to his reputation. Captain Trevelyan advised in such a quiet and suggestive manner that the old servant scarcely felt his growing inability. No discord prevailed. Moderation was the true secret. The family of Colonel Trevelyan treated their dependents with gentleness and kindness. Lady Trevelyan often sought advice from them in such a way as both showed her confidence in their opinion, and gained unbounded respect towards the relationship thus existing between them. Mary Douglas at first seemed inclined to shrink from the reserved demeanor of her ladyship, but further acquaintance made her feel comparatively at ease. Really the present occasion afforded opportunity for what may, with due propriety, be termed a complication of plans, or more properly still, plans within plans. Lady Trevelyan had formed her little plans. To do justice to her ladyship we will not say that she formed it, but that she would very agreeably and readily have acquiesced in the matter. Reader, we are half inclined to keep her ladyship's--no, we will not say plan--fond dream--a secret. Supposing that many of you are not considered temper-proof we dare not provoke the multiplied assaults of hitherto amiable and patient friends, therefore we will treat you fairly by taking you into our entire confidence at present. Lady Trevelyan had soon learned to love

Mary Douglas with a feeling akin to her nature. She fondly watched every effort or action in the movement of her favorite guest. Every playful or fond gesture was carefully hoarded up as a store of treasures in the mind of her ladyship. Faithfully did she note each mark of favor shown at the hand of the genial young host. Lady Trevelyan was ***only a woman*** as all others. Do not chide if she had set her heart upon one fond thought--if she secretly hoped that Guy Trevelyan would endeavor to secure for her another daughter in the beautiful Mary Douglas. Is a devoted mother always rewarded for such anxiety towards her first-born and heir? Do these respective heirs and highly-favored children strive to further the wishes of those deeply interested parents, especially mothers? In a more particular sense, did Captain Trevelyan take any steps to advance the scheme which lay near her ladyship's heart?

Fanny Trevelyan was also busily occupied in watching the daily progress of her fond projects. She was not overjoyed in fond expectation, yet was contented to await the result of daily companionship for an indefinite period, as Maude Bereford was to remain until her presence was demanded at the castle. Still the young hostess gave herself no uneasiness about her brother's affairs. If he would form an attachment to Maude Bereford it would be a source for much rejoicing and happiness. She was altogether unconscious of the counter plots or schemes laid to thwart her own. Mr. Howe was vastly entertaining in his endless variety of diverting moods, making himself by turn the especial cavalier of every lady in the company. To Lady Trevelyan he was doubly considerate and devoted. Captain Trevelyan knew the motive and warmly appreciated it. He had many times wished for an opportunity to return such passing acts of kindness, yet in vain. Captain Douglas fully sustained his former reputation for satirical jests and well-timed jokes at the expense of his friends. Frequently those whom he regarded ***most*** received attacks in proportion to the value of such regard. Formerly to Lieutenant Trevelyan and his friend Howe were daily administered doses of almost equal quantity and in double proportion to those outside the household. Yet who did not admire the gifted, manly, and handsome son of Sir Howard Douglas? Who was not ready to welcome him with heart and hand around the festive board or social circle? Who has not become infected by his jovial, gay, happy, and generous nature? Truly, Captain Charles Douglas was a worthy son of an honored race--the royal house of Douglas. In the midst of such a company of "tried friends and true," the days and weeks must have flown rapidly away while enjoying the hospitality of Trevelyan Hall.

Fanny Trevelyan, admired, petted, and caressed, had still the same childlike nature when friendship had been matured by daily companionship. Mary Douglas was charmed with the sweet and engaging manner which was at first attributed to a want of confidence. Frequently she spoke to Captain Trevelyan concerning his "child sister," as she playfully termed her once, exclaiming: "How beautiful if Fanny shall always be a child woman."

"It shall be my earnest wish," returned Guy; "I would not have her otherwise."

CHAPTER XX.
A WINTER IN THE ETERNAL CITY.

Gerald Bereford was now enjoying the soft summer breezes, blue skies and golden sunshine of an Italian climate. His health seemed to improve as he neared the far-famed city--the eternal city--the gigantic monument of what has been in ages of the mighty past. Many visions arose before Lady Rosamond's mind as she contemplated the magnificent ruins that met her at every gaze. In the company of several acquaintances they visited scenes of impressive and peculiar interest: St. Peter's, in all its glory, rising from its piazza of stately columns and fountains, something too grand for description. This imposing specimen of classic architecture, with grandeur inconceivable, the interior, the lofty dome, called up emotions her ladyship could never forget. In the coliseum the invalid seemed to enjoy returning vigor as he looked down from the upper halls and viewed the triumphal arches of Constantine, Septimus, Severus and Titus, now crumbling into decay, the lofty corridors left to the mercy of the elements, the endless porches grass grown and unprotected from the wild beast, the mouldering parapet, taught the one inspiring theme--mortality. This ruin of ruins--what can it not recall to a vivid imagination? The thousands who lined those seats in eager gaze upon the arena with its bloody and heart-sickening conflicts, its array of blood-thirsty antagonists, its dying groans, its weltering victims. Where are they? What remains? Awful solitude, awful grandeur, awful beauty, desolation. Peace, the emblem of Christianity, now reigns in the ancient stronghold of barbaric passion, butchery and strife. Lady Rosamond had visited ruins of palaces, castles, bridges, arches, cathedrals, monuments and countless relics of the past, but none had the power to chain her thoughts as the stupendous coliseum, viewed in the solemn stillness of a moonlight night. The present was a beautiful dream. It had a softening effect upon the devoted wife, infusing peace, content, and calm repose. The solemn reminders on every side had a charm to soothe her hitherto troubled breast. Holy emotions were nurtured within the heart where once reposed unresisting conflicts of rebellious strife and discontent.

With the warm breath of nature came awakening life into the emaciated frame of the invalid. Lady Rosamond devoted every waking moment to her husband. In the charming eventide they sat upon the balcony of their residence overlooking the Corso, catching a glimpse of the open country beyond the surrounding mountains and the ever restless Tiber. Frequently, they rode slowly along the Appian Way, now almost impassable for heaps of rubbish, mounds, and broken fragments, temples, columns, pillars, and successive piles of neglected relics. The Campagna, in its dreary aspect, often tempted their stay. Sometimes her ladyship would have a feeling of vexation, knowing that it was utterly impossible to visit more of the sights of Rome. They might remain for years and leave many scenes unexplored. The palace of the Vatican formed a life-long study for Lady Rosamond. Only a few of its four thousand rooms could be visited, yet these were bewildering in variety. Here they could view the most wonderful collections of art and grandeur that the world affords. Here were stored the endless piles of antique trophies of every clime--rooms representing oriental scenes throughout, starlit skies, and monsters of unknown existence meet one on every side and fill the mind with awe.

For the benefit of the reader we will insert the letters written by Lady Rosamond to her friend, Mary Douglas, containing a short description of some important places, and showing the tender interest inciting the writer when referring to the circumstance of her husband's ill health--the hopeful vein which pervaded throughout, and the true spirit of friendship extended to the absent one.

Rome, February 10th, 1831.

My Dearest Mary:

As many miles lie between us there is no alternative but the hastily written and imperfect scribble which will shortly be presented you, if the elements have not conspired against us.

In order to relieve your uneasiness I beg to state that Gerald's health is daily improving. He has much faith in Rome. Scarcely a day passes without his enjoying the benefit of the delightful atmosphere and the lovely drives out into the open country, of which I must tell you afterwards. The large number of acquaintances formed since our arrival have contributed much to our enjoyment. We frequently meet many of our old friends. Imagine our delightful surprise on seeing Captain Crofton, his wife and daughter. Of course you remember the latter--a lovely girl of purely blonde style, whom we meet at Lady Berkeley's, and who created such sensations in London circles on her first appearance in society. Gerald declares that the face of an old friend is better than medicine. What do you think he would say were you to enter rather suddenly upon us? My dearest, I know what I would say if such an overwhelming happiness were in store. These thoughts call up feelings which are inimical to peace and content. I am almost tempted to wish for the quiet of our English home and the sight of your dear face. But this must not be. I shall forget to give you some sights of Rome if I indulge in vain and foolish regrets. Really I am at a loss how to convey any idea of such scenes as we are almost daily witnessing. In the present instance I feel my inability to appreciate what is lofty and inspiring to every cultivated mind. Often I am inclined to envy those of brilliant intellectual perceptions like yourself. When the day arrives that you visit the Eternal City will it not be viewed in a different sense than in the present under the ordinary gaze of your short-sighted Rosamond?

Gerald says: "Tell Mary something of the churches," without thinking of the arduous task therein devolved. Poor fellow! He seems anxious to make amends for so much self-sacrifice. In compliance to his wishes your friend reaps twofold pleasure, therefore Mary shall hear "of the churches."

About three weeks ago a party of tourists, including the Croftons and ourselves; visited several of the grand old churches, so important in the history of Roman architecture of classic ages. The first we entered was the church of the Ara Coeli, said to occupy the site of the ancient temple of Jupiter Feretrius. It was a gloomy old structure with long rows of pillars of Etruscan design. On ascending the long flight of steep stairs on one side the impressive gloom increased. The situation awoke old associations of the sybilline and vague predictions of the time-honored soothsayers--their power--their greatness--their fall. We were more than impressed with the churches of St. Giovanni and St. Paolo, beneath which lay in awful depths the subterranean caverns said to be connected with the Coliseum. Gerald remained above while I followed the explorers through these dismal yawning gulfs seemingly ready to open and shut their victims in a living tomb. Streets ran in various directions; the mouldy, damp walls emitted a disagreeable watery vapor that rendered the air unbearable; stagnant pools lay on all sides. Is it not an appalling thought that these successive ranges of caverns were constructed for the human victims to be eaten by the beasts at the Coliseum, yet such is the legend. Doubtless you already weary of churches, but having first attempted them at the suggestion of Gerald, now I am deeply interested in the matter myself. But you will only listen to one more very short account. The church of San Sebastiano, which next received us, is situated on the Appian Way, and perhaps the most remarkable of any we have hitherto visited. The site is truly beyond description. The stupendous masses of rocks piled on every side appeared to give it an interest more than common. The endless rows of decaying columns, pillars, stained windows, and paintings, added one more link to the chain of daily events which form such an important part in our visit.

As I intend very soon to write you something of a livelier

description, I now conclude this hastily-written scribble. Dearest, I expect to hear from you all immediately. Gerald is rapidly improving, and is sanguine of ultimate recovery. Adieu. From

Your Rosamond.

Lady Rosamond now entertained hopes of her husband's recovery. He seemed much stronger and took a deeper interest in their explorations. In the company of English friends he visited all the accessible spots of historic ground. Lady Rosamond was always ready to encourage him by her hopeful remarks and winning smile. She had formed an attachment to the lovely Mabel Crofton, who indeed repaid her in a fond return.

Nothing gave Gerald Bereford more anxiety than the pale face of his wife. In his feeble health he strove to draw her ladyship's attention towards the social circle with a view to raise her occasional drooping spirits.

In the young English maiden Lady Rosamond found much company. They conversed much and enjoyed the sights together with united regard and interest.

In answer to a lengthy letter received shortly afterwards from Mary Douglas, the following was penned by Lady Rosamond:

Rome, April 15th, 1831.

My Darling Mary:

Truly did you respond to my wishes. How can I ever repay so much devotion? You have indeed granted my requests in mentioning all my friends, and giving all the matter which interests Gerald so much. He is indeed truly grateful and is going to write you by next mail. His health has not been improving so rapidly of late, yet we have every hope of his recovery. Will it not be a happy moment when we meet again on the shores of dear old England? The very dust and fog will have a charm hitherto unknown.

As we are in Rome you will expect something from Rome, therefore I

will tell you of what has recently been going on. Last week was the
Carnival. Gerald complained of weakness and fatigue, having exerted
himself too much during the previous week. He was much disappointed
in not being able to participate in the amusement, but had to be
satisfied by remaining on the balcony of our residence, overlooking
the Corso, which, as you know, is the principal street paraded on
those occasions. Gerald interrupts me by requesting a long letter
and full description, therefore on him alone rests the blame if I
exceed the length usually devoted to letter writing.

Now for the Carnival. At an early hour on Monday morning the usual
bustle and active preparations commenced. Carriages rolled along
laden with confectionaries and flowers. In fact the street, houses,
and passing vehicles of every description, appeared as though the
heavens had literally rained flowers--flowers showered in every
direction. Evidently we were certain that flowers were to be one of
the prominent features witnessed in the grand demonstration. Every
house opening on the Corso was covered with bright streamers,
pennons, and flags of every size, shape, color, and hue--red, blue,
white, green, gold, purple, yellow, and pink. Every window was
festooned with flowers, banners, and like array. Every shop was
converted into gorgeous saloons, decorated with trees, garlands,
evergreens, resplendent in silver, crimson, and gold, filled with
hundreds of anxious spectators. Every nook and corner was made
bright by the sparkle of beautiful eyes, merry smiles and happy
faces. Thousands jostled on every side in representation of
monkeys, lions, tigers, soldiers, clowns, maniacs. Satanic deities
and every other deity credited to countless ages, helped to swell
the crowd wedging themselves between line upon line of carriages
four abreast. The general bombardment commenced on all sides was
truly an exciting scene. Grand assaults were made upon houses and
carriage with alike furious resistance; missiles of bonbons rose in
the air, volley upon volley; storms of flowers. Those seated in

windows and balconies made desperate onsets upon the passing carriages. Hand to hand encounters now became general; monkeys assailed lions; mamelukes returned the fire of gipsies; a grand hurly-burly arose from every point in sight. Clouds fell from upper balconies upon each side of the street as the crowds poured on in incessant streams which became at intervals one moving mass of dust, white as snow. Beautiful ladies, maidens and children, mingled in the gay scene--all intent upon the same enjoyment. It is impossible to convey the faintest idea of this grand display which is kept up from early morning until half-past four o'clock, when the street is cleared as by magic. How such a concourse of carriages and people get into the adjoining nooks and piazzas in such a short time is astonishing, while thousands still cling to the sidewalks of the Corso. A chariot race is the next proceeding, when, within the space of a few moments, the horses are in their places--the signal given--the distance of the Corso gained--the race won.

This is the first day's outline of sport, which is followed in successive order until the end of the season. Having already lengthened this letter in twofold proportion, I must take room to say that the festive scene instantly ceases as the solemn notes of Ave Maria rises from the hundreds of steeples--the requiem for the departing carnival.

I will not distract your attention with the palaces of the Caesars, the Cenci, St. Angelo, and the remains of antiquity still to be seen here, but trust that when we meet again every wish that you formerly expressed regarding our stay in Rome will be realized a thousandfold.

Looking at the volume of this letter I feel quite ashamed, but trust that absence and distance will help to plead my cause. Gerald seems quite confident that his suggestion will also speak loudly in

my favor, and perhaps he is right. At least I hope so. Remember me
kindly to every one of the family, I shall mention none
particularly. Gerald expresses a wish not to be forgotten by you.
Now, dearest Mary, if this truly formidable missive weary you,
please deal gently with Gerald and

Your Loving Rosamond.

Lady Rosamond had given her friend some of the glimpses of her experience in
Rome, yet she had much more to relate on her arrival. Some months would elapse
before her husband would consider his health sufficiently restored to return to his
native land. At intervals he seemed almost restored when a sudden relapse would
cause a renewed return of the symptoms attending his flattering disease. Still they
were hopeful that with the returning spring health would be restored the patient
invalid. Throughout the severe dispensation Gerald Bereford manifested no irrita-
tion, no fretfulness, no complaining. He seemed to be happy in appreciating the
labors of his beautiful wife. On one occasion, when she asked if he did not weary of
his sickness, he quietly replied:

"Darling Rosamond, it has shown that you are willing to sacrifice every pleasure in devotion to one who can never fully repay such a debt of gratitude. Do you
think that I can try, my Rosamond?" exclaimed he, pressing a fond kiss upon the lips
of the pale but lovely woman, as she sat beside him.

Ah! Gerald Bereford knew not that in these words there lay a hidden meaning.
Surely, and in a way unknown to both, will the debt be paid.

CHAPTER XXI.
LIGHT, SHADOW, AND DARKNESS.

The guests at Trevelyan Hall had departed, Maude Bereford alone remaining. Captain Trevelyan applied himself to the duties devolving upon him with a will. His hospitality was the comment of many. He had begun life aright. His honest heart and upright principles were a sure passport to prosperity and popularity. "The Hall" was a scene of much gaiety and resort. Large gatherings were of frequent occurrence, to which the families of the surrounding neighbourhood were cordially invited. Fanny Trevelyan was idolized among her youthful companions and associates. Her sweet face was welcomed as a delightful acquisition on every occasion. Many sought to show their fond appreciation of her retiring manners and graceful elegance. Flattery had no power over her. She possessed a character of too much depth and penetration to harbor the least feeling akin to vanity. Lady Trevelyan had guarded her daughter's education and trained her with a view to set a proper estimate upon those qualities which ennoble and elevate the soul. Maude Bereford was a proper companion for Fanny Trevelyan. Their minds were in harmony, while the latter acted as a propelling power to force the aspirations of the other above their common flight. Lady Trevelyan was pleased with this companionship. Though she could not discern the brilliant genius and powers which characterized the beautiful Mary Douglas, there was much to admire in Maude Bereford. Captain Trevelyan was kind, amiable and attentive. He paid every mark of respect towards his gentle and loveable guest. Frequently they walked, chatted and rode together. Maude was pleased with the gentlemanly attentions of the engaging officer, and showed her appreciation in many ways. He enjoyed the society of those two girls much as those of playful children. Fanny was truly happy in her brother's company.

"Dear Guy, you must never love any one more than me," was a frequent rejoinder as she received his many tender caresses.

One day, when seated upon the lower end of the balcony, Fanny laid her hand lovingly upon her brother's shoulder and looking into his face, exclaimed:

"Guy, I have often wondered about you."

"About me, pet," returned the latter, "what can it be about me that is really worthy of so much attention from a young lady fair? Already I feel as of some importance."

Guy Trevelyan was now a handsome man of twenty-seven. The effeminate blush of youth had given place to an open and engaging animation that made him doubly attractive. Turning his gaze upon his sister, he added:

"Come, little one, tell me this great wonder. I must not be kept in suspense. Cannot Maude assist you? If so, I rely upon her in the present dilemma," said Guy, turning in playful appeal to Maude Bereford.

"Your surmise is groundless, ***mon frere***," returned Fanny, in childish glee, "Maude is entirely in the dark, (pardon the vulgarism.)"

"I will pardon you in everything, provided you gratify my curiosity," said the other.

"Fanny, it is unjust to treat Guy in this way," said Maude, by way of intercession.

"Two against one," cried Fanny, with a demure smile upon her face. "The majority has it. I am placed in a difficult position," said she, turning to her friend, adding, "Maude only for your suggestion I might have been able to extricate myself. Well, I shall try my best to maintain peace by compliance to your united wishes."

"By telling us one of the seven wonders," interrupted Maude.

"Yes," said Fanny, "I have often wondered why it was that Guy could remain so long in the companionship of Mary Douglas or Lady Rosamond and come back heart whole to Trevelyan Hall."

Captain Trevelyan had received a home thrust, yet he betrayed no feeling and showed no reason for suspicion, at least in the eyes of his sister and her companion. A quiet laugh greeted the remark. Guy Trevelyan had not the keen glances of the secretary levelled at him now, else the puzzling expression that rested awhile upon his face would instantly have been detected.

"That is the great wonder," said the brother, drawing his sister nearer to his side, adding: "Well, my little sister, until *you* have become weary of your brother's keeping he is anxious to claim the gracious liberty of possessing the love of one devoted heart. What says *la belle* Fanny?"

"Oh, Guy," cried Maude, "she was afraid that you may possibly have charitable intentions towards some fair one and wishes to make the test."

"Why, Maude," exclaimed Fanny, "you are really in earnest; I shall begin to think, from the stand you have taken in the matter, that Guy had better beware, else ere long he will not be able to make such avowals to his sister."

"Come, come, little mischief-maker, no jealousy," cried Captain Trevelyan, hastily drawing an arm of each within his own, and then they joined her ladyship in the shrubbery.

Fanny Trevelyan was truly in jest. She had found that no real attachment was to be formed between her brother and friend. There had arisen instead a tender familiarity, a friendship that is rare to be seen. Maude Bereford had grown to treat Guy Trevelyan with brotherly kindness. It pleased him to witness this feeling arising from disinterested friendship and motives of genuine purity. Were it otherwise he would feel an embarrassment that might affect his honest nature. When left to himself he could not dismiss from his thoughts the remark made by his sister. He knew she was ignorant of his affairs in New Brunswick, yet he felt sorely puzzled.

Not long after the following conversation took place, Maude Bereford was preparing to hasten homeward. Lady Rosamond sent cheerful accounts of her husband's rapid improvement. They were still visiting amid the ruins in hopes of speedily returning to England.

Every fortnight brought to Trevelyan Hall a lengthy epistle from Mary Douglas--lengthy from the fact of its being addressed to each member of the family--bearing remembrance to Lady Trevelyan, many choice bits of gossip to Guy, and charming effusions to Fanny, full of love and tenderness. Her last contained a glowing allusion to Lady Rosamond--an eager desire to meet her loving friend; also fervent gratitude for the hopeful restoration of Gerald's health.

"I am almost inclined to feel a pang of jealousy," exclaimed Fanny, as she read and re-read the contents of the precious missive. "Mary loves Lady Rosamond better than any other friends on earth."

"Why not, my child?" questioned Lady Trevelyan; "they are old friends--friends in childhood, girlhood, and womanhood. Lady Rosamond is worthy of the truest and purest love. She is beautiful, good, and lovable. Who could see her ladyship but to admire and love?"

"Dear Mamma," returned Fanny, "you share my sentiments towards Lady Rosamond. Guy seemed surprised when I ventured to wonder why he could remain so long in the daily society of two such gifted and lovely beings as her ladyship and Mary Douglas, without forming stronger ties than those of friendship."

"Both are lovely," exclaimed Lady Trevelyan. "It would indeed be a difficult matter for a lover to decide between two so much alike in beauty, grace, and loveliness."

"Strange that I did not think of this before, mamma," said the childlike Fanny with an air of much wisdom. "The poet must certainly have experienced the same predicament when he wrote:

\"How happy could I be with either,
Were t'other dear charmer away."

A week had elapsed after Maude had arrived at the castle when a hastily written note was received by Fanny Trevelyan from the former, containing sad news from Rome. Gerald Bereford had apparently recovered, and was on the eve of returning home when he was suddenly seized with hemorrhage of the lungs, which rapidly reduced him and brought on prostration. Medical assistance had been obtained, but he now lay in a critical state, every means being used to prevent another attack, in which case there could be no hope.

Maude Bereford had penned those lines in bitter anguish. She loved her brother from the depths of her heart. His life must be spared. Heaven could not deprive her of such a blessing. Ah, no, he will live! In this hour of trial the sorrowing girl sought comfort in those rebellious and sinful thoughts. She had not the sustaining faith to say, "Thy will be done." It is needless to say that Maude's letter met much sympathy at "The Hall." Fanny cried heartily. She could not think of any thing but the sadness that had fallen upon the inmates of the Castle.

"Poor Lady Rosamond," exclaimed she, in tones of undisguised sadness, "how she will lament her sad fate if Gerald should die? Oh, mamma, I cannot think it possible that he must die."

"Tempt not Heaven, my child, for 'with God all things are possible,'" said Lady Trevelyan, who was a truly Christian woman. "Everything is ordered aright," continued her ladyship, "there are no afflictions or trials in life but what are considered for our good. It is indeed a heavy blow upon the young wife to lose the husband of her choice, but how many have borne up when deprived of father, mother, husband and child."

"Oh, mamma," exclaimed Fanny, "if I could only look upon the ways of Providence in the same manner as you. I know it is sinful, but I cannot help thinking that it is too hard for Gerald to be taken away from Lady Rosamond. How I pity her. Poor dear Maude too. How badly she must feel."

The physician's worst fears were realized. Spite of every care and precaution a second attack of hemorrhage made its fatal ravages upon the fast sinking body of the sufferer. Gerald Bereford must die. All hopes are at an end. Death has set its seal upon his broad, fair forehead. Soon the eyes that still fondly linger upon the form of his beautiful wife shall close to open upon the scenes of another world.

This was a bitter trial to Lady Rosamond! Her husband was to die in a foreign land. He was to be deprived of a last farewell to the dear friends at home. Such thoughts, bore heavily upon the susceptible nature of this faithful woman. Could she then have gathered those loved ones around the dying bed of her husband, she would have sacrificed every earthly desire; yes, her life. Then did she think of her friend, Mary Douglas; then did she need the consolation of a true Christian friend. Like a ministering angel, she strove to soothe the last hours of her dying husband. Never was woman more devoted, heroic and patient. Not a murmur escaped her lips as she sat for hours watching the quickening breath in death-like struggle, convulsing the almost lifeless form of one who had ever been kind, dutiful, loving, and true to his vow.

On his death-bed, Gerald Bereford felt no pangs of remorse devouring his latest thoughts. He could die in the belief of having been ever devoted to her whom he had promised to love, cherish and protect. Keenly did Lady Rosamond feel this reflection. Had her husband been less kind, generous and true, she could have borne the present with a firmness worthy of her spirit. But the thoughts that now filled her breast were maddening, merciless and torturing.

"What have I done to suffer so much through life," was the mental question ever uppermost.

Gerald Bereford had fought the battle of life bravely. He had taken part in its conflicts and struggles, never flinching from his post when duty called. Ambition had dazzlingly tempted him on--on--further on. He must be victorious in gaining the cause for which so many had fought with firm determination. Could he have lived to see the result of such political warfare--its blessings and its privileges--its freedom--he might exclaim with the brave general, "I die happy." But he *did* die happy. He *lived* a happy life--he *died* a happy death.

Lady Rosamond had many kind friends amidst this sad bereavement. Her pale face had power to move the most stoical--more powerful than the loudest outbursts of grief, or the paroxysms of a passionate and unsubdued sorrow.

What she suffered in those hours of silent anguish Heaven alone can ever know. Thoughts forced themselves upon her almost too hard to bear. Truly did she need the strength for which she had prayed on a former occasion. It seems a sacrilegious intrusion to unveil the heart of this truly devoted woman, who had sacrificed her entire being to the wishes and welfare of one whom she had calmly laid to rest. Fain would we stop here. But the sequel must be told.

Lady Rosamond had married Gerald Bereford with a firm resolve to be a dutiful and yielding wife, yet her heart had refused to follow. She never loved the man who lived upon her smiles. Still he knew it not. She was to him kind, loving, and pure. She was indeed *kind*. In every action shone kindness in characters of bold relief. Everyone who knew her found naught but true kindness. *Loving*? Yes, loving; though Gerald Bereford stirred not the depths of Lady Rosamond's heart, she was capable of a love as undying as the soul that gave it birth. It was her life--her being. In pity for her faithful husband she had guarded every secret passage of the heart which might lead to the betrayal of bitter and desolate feelings. *Pure*? Yes; purity was the guiding star which marked the daily course of this woman's existence. Her acts were pure--her mind was pure--her heart was pure--every thought was pure. There was purity in her sorrow, leading to pure and holy thoughts--speaking to the soul--giving comfort--giving hope.

In deep sincerity did Lady Rosamond mourn for her husband. She mourned his loss as that of a loved brother--a dear friend--one in whom she confided. She found much comfort in the thought of having done her best. She had fulfilled her duty--she had struggled bravely. She had cheered her husband's path through life--she had kept her secret--made one being happy. Surely such thoughts must have offered some relief. She had committed no wrong, having gone forth at the summon of duty, she had taken upon her frail, trembling form, a cross overpowering in its weight, yet she murmured not.

As she is sitting beside the lifeless remains of one who had filled such an important part in her history--a striking illustration of life in its varied forms of existence--its joys--its sorrows--its longings--its aspirations--its dreams--let us look upon her as one of the many purified through much suffering--whose faith will meet its recompense.

CHAPTER XXII.
CONCLUSION.

Reader, we will ask you to follow us as we pass over a period of two years--two long years. The task imposed is an arduous one, yet, we shrink not. All former friends must be searched out, and once more introduced. Be not impatient if we do not succeed in the direct order of your wishes. In the uncertain distance faint echoes are already heard between intervals of solemn thoughts, while the name of Rosamond strikes upon our ear and vibrates within us as though the influence of myriads of spirits had woven around a deep subtle spell from which we cannot force ourselves. In truth, you have won us--your point is gained.

Now to your relief. Bereford Castle stands in its grandeur and beauty with not an object near to mar the effect. Its stoical exterior bears no impress of the loss sustained in the heir and son. Menacingly it frowns upon those scenes which recall the realities of life. Amid storm, sunshine, sickness and death, its aspect is unchanged--true type of its age, order and design. On entrance, the interior is calm, quiet and inviting. Daily contact with the inmates has had a soothing effect. Look around. In the spacious drawing room, opening upon the garden, is the family occupied in different ways. Lord Bereford is seated beside the familiar form of a beautiful woman dressed in robes of mourning. A second glance is not necessary to aid recognition. The sweet pensive smile is sufficient. Lady Rosamond has lost none of her charms. Time has no grudge against her for personal wrongs, no retributive justice to be meted out--instead, the quiet happiness of a contented mind is lavished with true delight. A fond light beams in the lovely eyes as they turn towards Maude Bereford--ever the same Maude that strolled around Trevelyan Hall some time in the past. The same simplicity is attached to every movement, action and speech--Maude still.

But a stranger is engrossing her attention. A tall, handsome and gallant gentleman occupies a seat at her side, devoting his attentions to her, occasionally addressing Lady Rosamond in terms of endearing familiarity. There is not much difficulty in ascertaining the relationship. Geoffrey Seymour had become a frequent visitor at the Castle. The blushes that greeted him told the tale upon Maude Bereford. Yet, she cared not for the eyes of the world. She had given her heart to a true, honorable and affectionate lover. Already she has woven bright dreams wherein are clearly portrayed outlines of two fond beings living in the sunshine of each other's love, surrounded by the comforts and ease of a bright and happy fireside. Lady Bereford is within the privacy of her own apartments. Grief and anxiety have left heavy marks upon her hitherto well preserved face. The furrowed forehead, wrinkles and grey hairs, show full well the heavy blow which had been dealt her ladyship in the death of her first-born. Time cannot eradicate the inroads made upon this high-minded woman. Her failing health speaks of dissolution. The mother's heart that beat so wildly as she dreamt of the glorious future of her son, now feebly responded to the sluggish torpor of faded hopes.

Other friends are awaited at the Castle. Ere we have time to turn aside, light steps are flying across the hall and a girlish figure is at our elbow, and the next instant in the arms of Lady Rosamond and Maude. The childish face of Fanny Trevelyan once seen is not soon to be forgotten. Oh no, Fanny, you occupy an important niche within our memory! Two years were only a myth--a dream to the young mistress of Trevelyan Hall, save when some other's troubles aroused her sympathy and called forth the fine feelings of her nature. The former playful glee is still alive in Fanny's buoyant and lively manner. Her gaiety at times subsides to gaze upon Lady Rosamond's thoughtful face. The heart of this maiden is still fancy free. Guy Trevelyan is not disappointed in his sister, he being yet the dearest object of her heart.

"Dearest Maude," cried Fanny, in rapturous delight, "will we not form a happy family when Mary joins us."

"One would consider you a happy family already if happiness bears comparison by merriment," ventured a well-known voice from the outside apartment--a voice that had power to stir the soul of Lady Rosamond to its lowest depths, and kindle the smouldering passion time had vainly tried to smother into a fierce and steady flame. Strange that her ladyship must pass another fiery ordeal--that she must add more sorrow to her hitherto sad, eventful life.

No quivering lip or trembling form gave hope to Guy Trevelyan as he pressed the small white hand of one whom he loved tenderly and passionately--one whose image had been engraven upon his memory since he had given his boyish affections to the lovely, high-born, gentle girl, when a guest at Government House in Fredericton. Like the last moments of a drowning man, scenes he had almost forgotten flashed before him in countless array--scenes, varied and infinite, in which Lady Rosamond formed the pleasing foreground.

Face to face with this beautiful woman Guy Trevelyan was ready to fall down in adoration and pour out the tale of his sorrow with the ardor of undying love. What is the tenor of his thoughts while engaged in quiet and easy conversation with her ladyship and the other occupants of the drawing-room? Guy Trevelyan is wondering if he dare avow his love--if by any means he can find hope to approach Lady Rosamond on a subject which engrosses his waking thoughts.

Mary Douglas completed the family circle. With her came love, joy, hope, and happiness. Her lovely presence gave fresh impulse to every one greeting her arrival. Lady Rosamond felt a ray of light shed upon her as she caressed her true and constant friend. Maude was happier, if possible, in the love of Geoffrey Seymour when listening to the sweet silvery voice of this peerless woman. Fanny was overjoyed on the arrival of Mary Douglas. She alone could open her heart before the gaze of a companion. Her affections were untrammelled by false hopes or unrequited love. She sought the society of the former with a feeling bordering on idolatry. Together they spent much of their time, while Captain Trevelyan was thrown upon the resources of Lady Rosamond. The constant companionship of the man whom she loved cost many a bitter struggle to her ladyship. The earnest gaze of Guy Trevelyan's soft eyes were indeed hard to bear. If he only knew the power thus exercised upon the fair being beside him. But Lady Rosamond had kept her secret from the eye of any living creature save herself. Captain Trevelyan must not discover the fatal knowledge. He must never know. Still they conversed together, talked together, and spent many hours together, having much opportunity to fathom the depths of each other's heart. Lady Rosamond seemed cheerful, content, and happy. Captain Trevelyan was apparently light-hearted, pleasing, agreeable, and attentive. Each guest endeavored to make the most of this friendly meeting. Even Lady Bereford strove to forget her feelings and rally her former spirits and dignified stateliness. Bereford Castle enjoyed a season of delight.

One lovely evening afterwards several voices mingled in the shrubbery adjoining the garden. Maude was conversing in animated tones with Fanny Trevelyan. Geoffrey Seymour had played truant to his lady love by gallant attention to Mary Douglas.

In a remote corner, almost beyond hearing of these, and scarcely visible through the foliage, were the forms of a lady and gentleman seated beneath the sheltering branches of a stately elm. A nearer approach shows the rising color of the rose-tinted cheeks--the glorious light in those lovely eyes--the bewitching and irresistible smile. A manly voice is heard exclaiming in the tones of a rapturous lover, "Rosamond, my own darling, I never expected to realize such happiness. In the possession of such love I am a thousandfold rewarded for a lifetime of misery. Yes, my peerless Rosamond, the last half hour has amply repaid the torturing pangs of a forlorn and hopeless love which I have suffered since first beholding you." At this avowal the speaker leaned towards Lady Rosamond Bereford, revealing the features of Captain Trevelyan. In a moment of passionate fervor he had confessed his undying attachment to the lovely Rosamond, and had received the blissful assurance of reciprocated love. He was in possession of a happiness beyond description as he told the oft repeated tale to his betrothed wife, listening to her voice as it fell like music upon his ear. The fond kiss which sealed their vows was more precious than the mines of Golconda. Truly did Guy Trevelyan idolize the beautiful woman who had now surrendered her heart to his keeping.

Did Lady Rosamond tell *her* secret to her accepted lover? Did she also confess the love which had been cherished towards the boyish lieutenant when he became almost a daily visitor at Government House--the maddening thoughts, that almost crushed her out of existence--the spirit of rebellion against the designs of her loved parents--her resolution made to Lady Douglas--her bitter struggle between duty and feeling--strength of character--victory over self--devotion to her husband?

This is *our* secret, and we will never reveal it. The reader must be content to know that Captain Trevelyan was made happy beyond expectation by whatever revelation or by what answer. Truly they were

"Two souls with but a single thought,
Two hearts that beat as one."

Let us assume the garb of the seer and step stealthily over the distance dividing the future, and gently draw aside the veil! What meets our gaze? A beautiful picture. The scene is now in Trevelyan Hall, where a reception is being held to welcome the beautiful bride of Captain Trevelyan--Lady Rosamond Trevelyan. Truly the peerless Rosamond. The beauty of the latter never shone so resplendent. Love has brought its unsurpassing charms. Love imparted life, brilliancy and soul to the face of the bride. Captain Trevelyan gazed upon her as though such radiance could scarcely be of earth. In the train of guests foremost stands Mary Douglas, whose happiness is indeed great. She is certain of the love existing between the newly-wedded pair, therefore reflects happiness from the thought. Next in order follows Maude Bereford, whose smiling face shows plainly the impress stamped upon her heart as she returns the gaze of her handsome betrothed, whose love is entirely devoted to her, save the tender attachment borne towards his sister Lady Rosamond Trevelyan. And our little favorite Fanny? Yes. Fanny Trevelyan is there in all her sweetness, engaging as ever, winning friends by every smile. Her joy is great. Lady Trevelyan's matronly grace and beauty appears to great advantage as she cast benign glances towards her daughter elect. Lady Rosamond in her eyes is a woman worthy to be loved--worthy of a mother's love. A group seated near, evidently in merry conversation, attracts our attention. One is entertaining them with something of a humorous character. The lively gestures and satirical smiles are certainly those of Captain Douglas. Doubtless he is telling of some sport which he enjoyed at the expense of Mr. Howe and Lieutenant Trevelyan in the field, barracks, or drawing-room, when in Fredericton. Charles Douglas, the handsome, brave, and generous son of Sir Howard, still proudly wears his former reputation unsullied and undimmed. His heart is ever ready to do an act of kindness for a fellow creature. Beloved, honored, and respected, he is worthy of his distinguished sire. Ah! we see another familiar form and face. Leaning beside an open window is that of a dear old friend, apparently occupied in studying the varied expressions of the happy bridegroom, and vainly trying to discover that puzzled one which had given so much concern on former occasions. The faithful friend of the young lieutenant of the 52nd has not forgotten to pay his respects to the retired captain of the 81st and his lovely bride. He had made a sacrifice to be present at an event which brought such happiness to one in whom he had always taken such a deep interest. Mr. Howe was indeed a happy, honored, and welcome guest. Many more are to be observed standing, sitting, reclining, in groups and companies; but as strange faces have no peculiar charm when feasting upon those of our old acquaintances, we make no effort to introduce them. In our great joy we had almost forgotten to recognize one of Lady Rosamond's warmest adherents--one always in attendance upon her ladyship, ready to engage in any fun, frolic, or excursion, in the direction of fields or woods--no less a personage than John Douglas; no longer important Johnnie, but a well-bred gentleman, hearty, jovial, merry, with bravery stamped upon every lineament of his face. Some are missing. Sir Thomas Seymour has not lived to see this. Lady Bereford is also among the number. She has paid her last debt.

Having brought before you most of those in whom you have no doubt became interested, we now bid them all a tender adieu. It is hard to part with friends who have shared our sorrow, our sympathy, and our joy, but in so doing may our prayers follow each throughout time, hallowed by fond memories of the past.

A second thought to Lady Rosamond before turning forever from the light of her lovely smile. In her great happiness there are moments when holy thoughts arise, having a purifying influence upon her life. She never can forget the past, while the present begets the consciousness of having trodden the paths of duty and right with firm, unfaltering steps, never looking back until the goal was reached--the reward gained.

"When life looks lone and dreary
What light can dispel the gloom?
When Time's swift wing grows weary
What charm can refresh his plume?
'Tis woman, whose sweetness beameth
O'er all that we feel or see;
And if man of heaven e'er dreameth
'Tis when he thinks purely of thee,
O woman!"

The Codes Of Hammurabi And Moses
W. W. Davies

QTY

The discovery of the Hammurabi Code is one of the greatest achievements of archaeology, and is of paramount interest, not only to the student of the Bible, but also to all those interested in ancient history...

Religion   **ISBN:** *1-59462-338-4*   **Pages:**132

MSRP $12.95

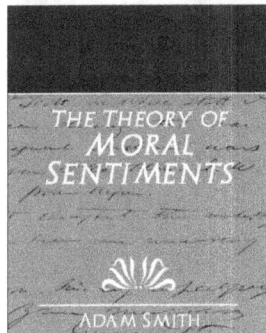

The Theory of Moral Sentiments
Adam Smith

QTY

This work from 1749. contains original theories of conscience amd moral judgment and it is the foundation for systemof morals.

Philosophy **ISBN:** *1-59462-777-0*   **Pages:**536

MSRP $19.95

Jessica's First Prayer
Hesba Stretton

QTY

In a screened and secluded corner of one of the many railway-bridges which span the streets of London there could be seen a few years ago, from five o'clock every morning until half past eight, a tidily set-out coffee-stall, consisting of a trestle and board, upon which stood two large tin cans, with a small fire of charcoal burning under each so as to keep the coffee boiling during the early hours of the morning when the work-people were thronging into the city on their way to their daily toil...

Pages:84

Childrens   **ISBN:** *1-59462-373-2*   *MSRP $9.95*

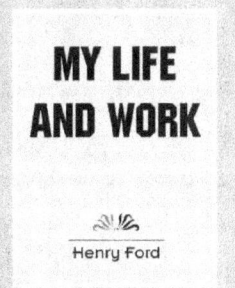

My Life and Work
Henry Ford

QTY

Henry Ford revolutionized the world with his implementation of mass production for the Model T automobile. Gain valuable business insight into his life and work with his own auto-biography... "We have only started on our development of our country we have not as yet, with all our talk of wonderful progress, done more than scratch the surface. The progress has been wonderful enough but..."

Pages:300

Biographies/   **ISBN:** *1-59462-198-5*   *MSRP $21.95*

The Art of Cross-Examination
Francis Wellman

QTY

I presume it is the experience of every author, after his first book is published upon an important subject, to be almost overwhelmed with a wealth of ideas and illustrations which could readily have been included in his book, and which to his own mind, at least, seem to make a second edition inevitable. Such certainly was the case with me; and when the first edition had reached its sixth impression in five months, I rejoiced to learn that it seemed to my publishers that the book had met with a sufficiently favorable reception to justify a second and considerably enlarged edition. ..

Pages:412

Reference   ISBN: *1-59462-647-2*   *MSRP $19.95*

On the Duty of Civil Disobedience
Henry David Thoreau

QTY

Thoreau wrote his famous essay, On the Duty of Civil Disobedience, as a protest against an unjust but popular war and the immoral but popular institution of slave-owning. He did more than write—he declined to pay his taxes, and was hauled off to gaol in consequence. Who can say how much this refusal of his hastened the end of the war and of slavery ?

Law   ISBN: *1-59462-747-9*   **Pages:48**

MSRP $7.45

Dream Psychology Psychoanalysis for Beginners
Sigmund Freud

QTY

Sigmund Freud, born Sigismund Schlomo Freud (May 6, 1856 - September 23, 1939), was a Jewish-Austrian neurologist and psychiatrist who co-founded the psychoanalytic school of psychology. Freud is best known for his theories of the unconscious mind, especially involving the mechanism of repression; his redefinition of sexual desire as mobile and directed towards a wide variety of objects; and his therapeutic techniques, especially his understanding of transference in the therapeutic relationship and the presumed value of dreams as sources of insight into unconscious desires.

Pages:196

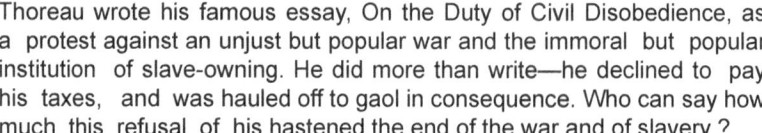

Psychology   ISBN: *1-59462-905-6*   *MSRP $15.45*

The Miracle of Right Thought
Orison Swett Marden

QTY

Believe with all of your heart that you will do what you were made to do. When the mind has once formed the habit of holding cheerful, happy, prosperous pictures, it will not be easy to form the opposite habit. It does not matter how improbable or how far away this realization may see, or how dark the prospects may be, if we visualize them as best we can, as vividly as possible, hold tenaciously to them and vigorously struggle to attain them, they will gradually become actualized, realized in the life. But a desire, a longing without endeavor, a yearning abandoned or held indifferently will vanish without realization.

Pages:360

Self Help   ISBN: *1-59462-644-8*   *MSRP $25.45*

QTY

The Rosicrucian Cosmo-Conception Mystic Christianity *by Max Heindel*   ISBN: 1-59462-188-8   **$38.95**
The Rosicrucian Cosmo-conception is not dogmatic, neither does it appeal to any other authority than the reason of the student. It is: not controversial, but is: sent forth in the, hope that it may help to clear...   New Age/Religion Pages 646

Abandonment To Divine Providence *by Jean-Pierre de Caussade*   ISBN: 1-59462-228-0   **$25.95**
"The Rev. Jean Pierre de Caussade was one of the most remarkable spiritual writers of the Society of Jesus in France in the 18th Century. His death took place at Toulouse in 1751. His works have gone through many editions and have been republished...   Inspirational/Religion Pages 400

Mental Chemistry *by Charles Haanel*   ISBN: 1-59462-192-6   **$23.95**
Mental Chemistry allows the change of material conditions by combining and appropriately utilizing the power of the mind. Much like applied chemistry creates something new and unique out of careful combinations of chemicals the mastery of mental chemistry...   New Age Pages 354

The Letters of Robert Browning and Elizabeth Barret Barrett 1845-1846 vol II   ISBN: 1-59462-193-4   **$35.95**
by Robert Browning and Elizabeth Barrett   Biographies Pages 596

Gleanings In Genesis (volume I) *by Arthur W. Pink*   ISBN: 1-59462-130-6   **$27.45**
Appropriately has Genesis been termed "the seed plot of the Bible" for in it we have, in germ form, almost all of the great doctrines which are afterwards fully developed in the books of Scripture which follow...   Religion/Inspirational Pages 420

The Master Key *by L. W. de Laurence*   ISBN: 1-59462-001-6   **$30.95**
In no branch of human knowledge has there been a more lively increase of the spirit of research during the past few years than in the study of Psychology, Concentration and Mental Discipline. The requests for authentic lessons in Thought Control, Mental Discipline and...   New Age/Business Pages 422

The Lesser Key Of Solomon Goetia *by L. W. de Laurence*   ISBN: 1-59462-092-X   **$9.95**
This translation of the first book of the "Lernegton" which is now for the first time made accessible to students of Talismanic Magic was done, after careful collation and edition, from numerous Ancient Manuscripts in Hebrew, Latin, and French...   New Age/Occult Pages 92

Rubaiyat Of Omar Khayyam *by Edward Fitzgerald*   ISBN:1-59462-332-5   **$13.95**
Edward Fitzgerald, whom the world has already learned, in spite of his own efforts to remain within the shadow of anonymity, to look upon as one of the rarest poets of the century, was born at Bredfield, in Suffolk, on the 31st of March, 1809. He was the third son of John Purcell...   Music Pages 172

Ancient Law *by Henry Maine*   ISBN: 1-59462-128-4   **$29.95**
The chief object of the following pages is to indicate some of the earliest ideas of mankind, as they are reflected in Ancient Law, and to point out the relation of those ideas to modern thought.   Religion/History Pages 452

Far-Away Stories *by William J. Locke*   ISBN: 1-59462-129-2   **$19.45**
"Good wine needs no bush, but a collection of mixed vintages does. And this book is just such a collection. Some of the stories I do not want to remain buried for ever in the museum files of dead magazine-numbers an author's not unpardonable vanity..."   Fiction Pages 272

Life of David Crockett *by David Crockett*   ISBN: 1-59462-250-7   **$27.45**
"Colonel David Crockett was one of the most remarkable men of the times in which he lived. Born in humble life, but gifted with a strong will, an indomitable courage, and unremitting perseverance...   Biographies/New Age Pages 424

Lip-Reading *by Edward Nitchie*   ISBN: 1-59462-206-X   **$25.95**
Edward B. Nitchie, founder of the New York School for the Hard of Hearing, now the Nitchie School of Lip-Reading, Inc, wrote "LIP-READING Principles and Practice". The development and perfecting of this meritorious work on lip-reading was an undertaking...   How-to Pages 400

A Handbook of Suggestive Therapeutics, Applied Hypnotism, Psychic Science   ISBN: 1-59462-214-0   **$24.95**
by Henry Munro   Health/New Age/Health/Self-help Pages 376

A Doll's House: and Two Other Plays *by Henrik Ibsen*   ISBN: 1-59462-112-8   **$19.95**
Henrik Ibsen created this classic when in revolutionary 1848 Rome. Introducing some striking concepts in playwriting for the realist genre, this play has been studied the world over.   Fiction/Classics/Plays 308

The Light of Asia *by sir Edwin Arnold*   ISBN: 1-59462-204-3   **$13.95**
In this poetic masterpiece, Edwin Arnold describes the life and teachings of Buddha. The man who was to become known as Buddha to the world was born as Prince Gautama of India but he rejected the worldly riches and abandoned the reigns of power when...   Religion/History/Biographies Pages 170

The Complete Works of Guy de Maupassant *by Guy de Maupassant*   ISBN: 1-59462-157-8   **$16.95**
"For days and days, nights and nights, I had dreamed of that first kiss which was to consecrate our engagement, and I knew not on what spot I should put my lips..."   Fiction/Classics Pages 240

The Art of Cross-Examination *by Francis L. Wellman*   ISBN: 1-59462-309-0   **$26.95**
Written by a renowned trial lawyer, Wellman imparts his experience and uses case studies to explain how to use psychology to extract desired information through questioning.   How-to/Science/Reference Pages 408

Answered or Unanswered? *by Louisa Vaughan*   ISBN: 1-59462-248-5   **$10.95**
Miracles of Faith in China   Religion Pages 112

The Edinburgh Lectures on Mental Science (1909) *by Thomas*   ISBN: 1-59462-008-3   **$11.95**
This book contains the substance of a course of lectures recently given by the writer in the Queen Street Hall, Edinburgh. Its purpose is to indicate the Natural Principles governing the relation between Mental Action and Material Conditions...   New Age/Psychology Pages 148

Ayesha *by H. Rider Haggard*   ISBN: 1-59462-301-5   **$24.95**
Verily and indeed it is the unexpected that happens! Probably if there was one person upon the earth from whom the Editor of this, and of a certain previous history, did not expect to hear again...   Classics Pages 380

Ayala's Angel *by Anthony Trollope*   ISBN: 1-59462-352-X   **$29.95**
The two girls were both pretty, but Lucy who was twenty-one who supposed to be simple and comparatively unattractive, whereas Ayala was credited, as her Bombwhat romantic name might show, with poetic charm and a taste for romance. Ayala when her father died was nineteen...   Fiction Pages 484

The American Commonwealth *by James Bryce*   ISBN: 1-59462-286-8   **$34.45**
An interpretation of American democratic political theory. It examines political mechanics and society from the perspective of Scotsman James Bryce   Politics Pages 572

Stories of the Pilgrims *by Margaret P. Pumphrey*   ISBN: 1-59462-116-0   **$17.95**
This book explores pilgrims religious oppression in England as well as their escape to Holland and eventual crossing to America on the Mayflower, and their early days in New England...   History Pages 268

www.bookjungle.com *email: sales@bookjungle.com fax: 630-214-0564 mail: Book Jungle PO Box 2226 Champaign, IL 61825*

QTY

The Fasting Cure *by Sinclair Upton*   ISBN: *1-59462-222-1*   **$13.95**
In the Cosmopolitan Magazine for May, 1910, and in the Contemporary Review (London) for April, 1910, I published an article dealing with my experi-
ences in fasting. I have written a great many magazine articles, but never one which attracted so much attention... New Age/Self Help/Health Pages 164

Hebrew Astrology *by Sepharial*   ISBN: *1-59462-308-2*   **$13.45**
In these days of advanced thinking it is a matter of common observation that we have left many of the old landmarks behind and that we are now pressing
forward to greater heights and to a wider horizon than that which represented the mind-content of our progenitors...   Astrology Pages 144

Thought Vibration or The Law of Attraction in the Thought World   ISBN: *1-59462-127-6*   **$12.95**
by William Walker Atkinson   *Psychology/Religion Pages 144*

Optimism *by Helen Keller*   ISBN: *1-59462-108-X*   **$15.95**
Helen Keller was blind, deaf, and mute since 19 months old, yet famously learned how to overcome these handicaps, communicate with the world, and
spread her lectures promoting optimism. An inspiring read for everyone...   Biographies/Inspirational Pages 84

Sara Crewe *by Frances Burnett*   ISBN: *1-59462-360-0*   **$9.45**
In the first place, Miss Minchin lived in London. Her home was a large, dull, tall one, in a large, dull square, where all the houses were alike, and all the
sparrows were alike, and where all the door-knockers made the same heavy sound...   Childrens/Classic Pages 88

The Autobiography of Benjamin Franklin *by Benjamin Franklin*   ISBN: *1-59462-135-7*   **$24.95**
The Autobiography of Benjamin Franklin has probably been more extensively read than any other American historical work, and no other book of its kind
has had such ups and downs of fortune. Franklin lived for many years in England, where he was agent...   Biographies/History Pages 332

Name	
Email	
Telephone	
Address	
City, State ZIP	

☐ **Credit Card**   ☐ **Check / Money Order**

Credit Card Number	
Expiration Date	
Signature	

Please Mail to: Book Jungle
PO Box 2226
Champaign, IL 61825
or Fax to: 630-214-0564

ORDERING INFORMATION

web: *www.bookjungle.com*
email: *sales@bookjungle.com*
fax: *630-214-0564*
mail: *Book Jungle PO Box 2226 Champaign, IL 61825*
or PayPal *to sales@bookjungle.com*

Please contact us for bulk discounts

DIRECT-ORDER TERMS

**20% Discount if You Order
Two or More Books**
Free Domestic Shipping!
Accepted: Master Card, Visa,
Discover, American Express